# Hunting Jackars

## The Chronicles of Datch

## By David Hallam

ISBN: 978-1-917238-18-2

# DEDICATION

For Emma.

## ACKNOWLEDGMENTS

I want to say thank you to all the staff in my local public house for putting up with me sitting in the corner typing away on my laptop.

I would also like to thank Mick the Hat for all his help with proof reading, I did spell something right somewhere, I'm just not sure which book it was in.

Also, I would like to thank Google's Bard, I used the AI for gramma checking and very good it was too.

# Starlight

Datch and The Pack were on their fifth galactic tour. This included their new recruit 'Kristina' who had changed her name to Krissy after she had decided it sounded cooler. Datch and Carina had picked her up while on honeymoon when they were hanging out on a planet called Earth looking for ice cream. They were made to take her home with them by the IPSF after uploading the Bellatrixian language matrix into her head so they could talk to her. After which they were unable to remove it. They did however discover that she could sing and as Jep was leaving to become a chat show host, she took his place in the band. This had also meant that the girls were now doing their own song with the boys giving them backing vocals. Datch and Carina had sorted out an implant for her as well as giving her a room at their house. During the past year she had fitted in very well with The Pack and had rapidly become a big part of the family.

The Pack were in the star lounge on Zenoss five's orbital station, Starlight. They were on the station waiting for the Raven to be refuelled. This was due to the next system on the current tour being five hundred light years from the last one and the Raven only had a four hundred light year range. The Zenoss system was a little over halfway between the two and they had taken the opportunity to stretch their legs on the station while the ship was being resupplied.

The station itself was a massive cylindrical structure with the docking bays in the centre. The docking bays had huge lifts that took the ships deep inside the station, taking both people and cargo to the main habitation and operations areas. This was on the inside edge of the hull and had normal gravity for Zenoss which was about nine tenths of Bellatrix. There were parks, forests, and fields inside the massive structure with buildings that stretched towards the centre separating all the areas. There were open air bars and cafés and even a large swimming pool. Entrances disappeared down into the lower levels where the cheaper habitation was as they had been built into parts of the hull.

The Pack's gigs were four weeks apart and they were on route to a star system near to the next gig for a nice long vacation. They had skipped a stop planet side because the beach resort on Hybaysus sounded much more fun than Zenoss. The world below was a water world and only had a small land mass with most of the populated areas being in domes under the oceans. Therefore, an eight hour stop over on the station with a nice long walk and a trip to a restaurant, sounded like a great idea. The Raven was a nice ship with a lot of luxuries but could be a bit claustrophobic at times especially when you consider the amount of the space inside her wasn't much bigger than a twelve-bed motel. There was no place for you to have your own space apart from in your bedroom.

The star lounge was on the end of the station and looked out over the planet below.

Datch was sitting gazing out of the window at the stars and the blue sparkling world laid out below when the girls came back from the shops. They were each carrying a large bag apart from Carina who had two.

"Hi guys, we found a great shopping mall on section seven." Said Carina triumphantly as she came walking over to the table.

Datch turned to her.

"Hi Babes, did you get anything nice?" he asked.

"Yes, we got some new clothes, souvenirs and a bag full of cookies."

Datch decided that cookies sounded good.

"Cookies?"

"Yes, they had a large range, so we got a bag full of different types. We can put them in storage and eat them on the way to the next star system." She said waving one of the bags and letting the smell of fresh cookies waft around the area.

"Sounds like cookies for breakfast then." said Datch with a grin.

"Breakfast, I was thinking more like lunch. Anyway, you guys ready to head back?"

"Err, Let's just have one more drink before we leave and then we can have a coffee in that café on the way back."

"OK. Sounds good. How long is the next leg of the trip?"

"About three days. Then we hit the beach."

"Sounds good to me. Three weeks of doing nothing."

"I might get bored." Said Dapo.

Datch picked up his vid com and asked it about the resort and started to read it out.

"It says here that there is swimming, snorkelling, fishing, various beach games, indoor Solar Ball court, music as well as a number of other daily activities."

"Are there any shops near the resort?" Asked Rosey.

"There is a small village with some souvenir shops. At least that's what it says here, and it looks like a couple of other shops as well." Said Datch scrolling down his vid com.

"Cool. I think a bit of retail therapy maybe called for." Added Tish.

"You've just come back from the shops." Said Dapo.

Tish gave him a hard stare.

"It will be a nice relaxing shopping experience at the resort which is not the same as on a space station" She added still staring and Dapo.

They got another round of drinks and sat chatting for a while and then decided it was time to head back to the Raven via a café that was next to the docking area.

They left the bar and headed towards the lifts on the way to docking bays. They had got halfway to the lifts when there was a loud scream from down the corridor. Datch and Dapo ran around the corner to see what was going on. Two men were fighting with a young woman.

"Hey! What are doing?" shouted Datch.

The two men looked at him and then pushed the woman to the floor before running off. Datch and Dapo reached her and helped her to get up.

"Are you ok?" asked Datch just as the rest of The Pack caught them up.

"Yes, I think so." said the woman.

"Come and sit down over here." said Carina pointing at some seats just up the corridor a little way.

The woman followed her to the seating and sat down.

She looked quite pale and visibly shaken.

"What happened?"

"I was just walking back to my room on level four when the two men approached me and grabbed me."

"Well, they have gone now."

"Where is my bag?" she asked.

They looked around but the corridor was empty apart from a few piles of dust.

"I can't see it anywhere. Those men must have taken it."

"I'll go and call station security." said Fred and headed over to a coms panel.

"Oh, all my things were in my bag."

"Don't worry, I'm sure they can be replaced."

A look of horror crossed her face.

"Are you sure you're alright?" asked Carina.

"They've taken my Jackar." she said looking very upset.

"Your Jackar, What's a Jackar?"

"My Jackar is my soul. On my world we are all given a Jackar at birth. It symbolises our soul. We carry it with us through life until we find a partner and swap Jackars when we become joined."

"Oh. Well, hopefully the security services will catch them." said Datch.

Just then two security officers came running down the corridor.

"Over here officers." said Fred.

They came over to them and the taller of the two officers spoke.

"Hello all. We were told that someone had been assaulted and their things taken."

"Yes officer, it was me." said the woman.

"Hello mam, are you ok?"

"Yes, I'm OK, just a little shaken."

"When did it happen?"

"About five minutes ago."

He turned to the other officer.

"Can you pull the vid logs for this area."

He turned back to the woman.

"Can you tell us what happened?"

"I was just walking back to level four when two men approached me and grabbed me. Luckily, these kind people ran over to help me and the two men ran off taking my bag with them."

"Was there anything valuable in the bag?"

"Err, there was my vid com and my Jackar along with a few other bits."

"Your Jackar. Oh, that does make it a higher priority."

"Please can you get it back for me? I will be lost without it."

"We will try our best mam."

He turned to Datch and The Pack.

"Can you folks describe what happened?"

Datch explained about hearing the scream and running over to help the woman.

"Ok. let me do a quick scan of you all for our records please."

The officer started to scan everyone's ID and then stopped at the woman.

"Sorry mam, I didn't know who you were. My apologies. We will get you items back don't worry."

He turned to the other officer.

"Tell command we have Princess Deena from the Thoth star system here."

He turned back to the Princess.

"Your highness, why didn't you say who you were when I arrived?"

"I don't know. I'm sort of incognito."

"Ok, but where is your security detail."

"My two minders are sleeping. I've sort of err… sneaked out."

"That was a very dangerous thing to do your highness."

"Yes, I see that now. Thanks to these people I'm safe though."

Just then four more security officers came running down the corridor.

The Princess was calming down now. She turned to Datch.

"What are your names by the way?"

"I'm Datch and this my wife Carina."

Datch then introduced the other members of The Pack.

"I want to thank you all."

"You're welcome your highness."

"It was very lucky you were here. Where are you from?"

"We are from the Bellatrix star system that is about nine hundred light years from here."

"Wow, you're a long way from home."

All her colour had returned now, and she was sounding normal.

"Yes, we are a rock band and are currently doing and galactic tour."

"How very interesting. Are you going anywhere near Thoth?"

"I think we are in the star system next door for a number of gigs, but I don't think we have one in Thoth."

"I'll have to come over and see you perform."

"Sorry to interrupt you, your highness, but can we move you out of the corridor to somewhere safer."

"Oh yes officer, of course."

"Please if you would like to follow me. If the rest of you can come as well, we'll need to download your memories of the incident."

"Certainly officer, no problem." said Datch.

They followed the officer and the princess to the security office.

The security office was an oval room painted a light blue. At the far end was a desk with a set of double doors next to it. The room had a number of seats which were set out in small groups with small clear dividing panels in between them and were spread evenly around the room. The officer led the way through the doors next to the desk and down another short corridor to another room with more chairs in. These looked slightly better quality than the ones in the main room. There was also a drinks machine in the corner.

"If you would like to wait here, I'll prepare the implant reader and then can all of you that witnessed the attack come one at a time so that I can download the information we need. Please feel free to help yourselves to a drink while you wait."

They all sat down and waited. Then one at a time they were asked to go with the officer.

It came to Datch's turn. He got up and followed the officer across the corridor to the room opposite. The room had a control panel in one corner and a piece of equipment sitting in the middle with some sort of antenna structure pointing at a chair in front of it.

"OK, if you would like to sit in this chair, please."

Datch walked over and after inspecting the chair, sat down slowly. It was comfortable enough but had two padded sections that came out either side of your head so it was kept in one position.

"Will I feel anything?" he asked.

"No. You will see a box appear in your mind telling you a download is in progress and the period of the data being download. It will also show you time until complete. Other than that, it will be all over in a matter of a few seconds."

He pressed a few buttons and the antenna structure lowered itself to a few centimetres from Datch's head.

"Are you ready?"

"Yes sir."

The officer pressed a couple more buttons and a green light started flashing. Then after a few moments a box appeared in Datch's mind. It had a red flashing border with 'Download in progress'. Underneath it was a start and finish time that was showing the last twenty minutes and below that was a progress bar. The bar slowly turned to green and then the box vanished.

"OK, all done, sir." said the officer.

"Wow that was fast. Can anyone do that?"

"Well, if they had the right equipment but the signal is so small that they would have to get extremely close to you for it to work. The equipment is also classified and therefore you just can't go out and buy it off the shelf."

"Oh, I was worried in case people could hack into my memories."

"Well. One, you would know they were doing it and two, the implant only stores the last twenty-four hours. The rest of your information is stored on your external storage device or in your own memory. Only you can give access to that so no one can hack it. OK, if you would like to follow me back to the waiting room."

This put Datch's mind at ease and he followed the officer out of the door. They entered the waiting room.

'*What is it like?*' said Carina's voice in his head.

'*It's fine babes. You don't feel a thing when they do it.*' He thought back to her.

'*I was a little worried.*'

'*They just downloaded the attack bit, that's all.*'

'*Well, as long as you're ok.*'

Datch sat back down next to her.

"Yes." he said.

The officer took Dapo to the room for his download.

"Your highness. How come you left your bodyguards behind?" asked Carina.

"To be honest. I just get fed up with having my every moved watched and being told when and where to go. Being a princess is not all you would think it is. I'm a prisoner of the title."

"Don't you get time to yourself?"

"No, my bodyguards are always there. They even have a room next to mind at the palace. As soon as I get up, they are at my side."

"Wow. That must really be annoying." said Datch.

"Yes, very."

"Your highness, don't they let you do anything on your own?"

"Only if I'm within the palace and the area is secured. Can you please call me Deena? I know I'm a Princess but I just want to be plain Deena for a while."

Datch was quiet for a while and then came up with an idea.

"How are you getting home Deena?"

"We have a suite booked on a star liner in a couple of day's time, why?"

"Well, we have a spare couple of rooms on our ship. We also have a Solar Ball system in the hold and our own bar in the rec room. You would be welcome to join us."

"That is a very kind offer. I'm not sure my two bodyguards would like it though."

"Well, it would be safer than the star liner and faster. Our ship is armed and has a device that makes it pretty much invisible to other ships."

"Wow. That's quite impressive for a ship. Where did you get it from?"

"The President of our world gave it to Datch after we saved him and fixed Welly Four." Said Carina.

"Fixed Welly Four. You are the ones that ended the darkness?"

"Err… Yes, sort of." said Datch going a bit red.

"That is amazing. I am very honored to meet you."

"Thank you, Princess, I mean Deena."

"Look, maybe I can talk my bodyguards in letting me come with you. I would love to hear about what happened to Welly first hand."

Just then the officer came back in with Dapo.

"Hello, again. Thanks for all your help. We have identified the two men in question. One is a wanted outlaw whereas the second is a petty thief. We are currently searching the station for them. The sensors have tracked them to the docking area but because of the number of people coming and going, we are having trouble finding them. Can I suggest you stay on this level until we can locate them?"

"So, how long do you think it will take?"

"Maybe a couple of hours. Your highness, I can have a number of officers escort you to your room if you wish."

"Would it be ok if I stayed with these people? That's if its ok with you." she said turning to look at Datch who nodded.

"If you wish but I can't spare any officers to stay with you."

"That's ok officer, we'll make sure she is safe." said Datch.

At that point Datch's vid com beeped. It was Timbo telling him the Raven was refuelled and he had restocked the supplies. Mainly the beer. He told Timbo to meet them in the bar as soon as he could.

He turned back to the officer.

"We have Timbo coming now so it will take a small army to get to her."

"Ok. I'll escort you to the bar and then contact you when we have caught them."

"Thank you, officer. Could you contact my bodyguards and inform them where I am?"

"Yes, your highness. Now if you would all like to follow me."

They followed the officer out of the security office and back to the bar they were in earlier.

The bar was a large semi circler room with the bar at the centre. It was also quiet at the moment with quite a lot of empty tables dotted about. The bar had a large, raised area to one side. It was separated from the rest of the bar by a line of small posts and transparent panels. As they walked in, Timbo was standing at the bar taking up a large part of it. He noticed them come in and walked over to them.

"Hi Timbo."

"Hi Datch."

"Timbo, this is Princess Deena. We stopped some men from harming her and now are going to look after her for a while until it's safe."

"Hello your highness." He said and gave a little bow that looked more like a building bending over.

"It's just Deena, Timbo. And I'm please to meet you."

"Ok, Deena."

"Shall we go and sit down." Said Carina.

"Yes, the seats over there are free." Said Rosey.

The officer looked up at Timbo then up a bit more to find his face.

"Err, I can see your in safe hands your highness. I shall go and inform your bodyguards where you are."

"Thank you, officer."

"You're welcome your highness."

With that he left the bar.

Datch looked around the bar and spotted an area of seating which was a bit more enclosed than the rest and decided it would be safer for the Princess there. They followed Datch over and sat down. When everyone had got themselves sorted, they ordered a round of drinks.

"So, what is your music like?" Deena asked.

"We're a rock band and our music is, Well, quite loud. We sing songs like supernova and Star Lovers." said Carina.

"I think I've heard Star Lovers."

"Also, as you can see, we're glowing. That was a gift from Welly Four."

"Oh yes, Welly four. What happened there?"

Datch and The Pack went on to explain about Welly four. After about thirty minutes two women came walking in through the door and looked across at them. Datch had spotted them coming in as he was facing towards the door.

"Timbo."

Timbo stood up blocking most of the view.

The two women came walking over and then looked at Timbo. He smiled at them and shook his head. One of them tried to put her head around Timbo's arm and found out she needed a longer neck and went for saying in a loud voice.

"Your Highness?"

Deena got up and looked around Timbo.

"Hello." she said and turned to Timbo.

"It's ok Timbo. They're my bodyguards."

Timbo looked at them thoughtfully for a moment.

"Couldn't you have got bigger ones?" he asked as he stepped to the side so they could pass.

The two women went across to Deena and bowed.

"Are you OK your highness. We were told you had been assaulted?"

"Yes, I'm fine thanks to these wonderful people."

"With all due respect your highness, you should not have gone out without at least one of us by your side."

"I know. But I was fed up with never being on my own and thought it would be ok just to go for a little walk."

"We are going to have to inform your farther about this."

"I'm not so sure that would go down well. After all you were not with me." she said.

They looked at each other. The Princess was right. The king would not be happy about the fact they let her out of their sight and therefore were unable prevent the attack.

"Well, your highness. We had better hope the security force get your Jackar back. If they don't your farther will want to know how you lost it."

"I'm sure they will. Anyway, let me introduce you to my new friends."

Deena then proceeded to go around The Pack introducing them to the bodyguards. After which they sat down next to her. They would normally guard the entrance however, there was a Timbo in the way. It would be almost impossible to get passed him unless you were driving a tank and even that was a subject of debate.

"These kind people have offered to take us to the planetary system next to ours." Deena said.

"I'm sure they are very nice people but your itinerary lists you as going on the liner." Said the bodyguard, "We can't just go getting lifts off of strangers."

"Well, I think it would be a good idea as it would mean we were not in public view unlike onboard the liner."

"Yes, your highness, but we don't know them."

"Hmm, But I think we should." said Deena.

The bodyguard though about it for a moment and then came to a decision.

"OK, but we must do a full security check on all of them."

"I'm sure you will be happy with our checks. We have the top clearance on our home world and the president on speed dial." said Fred.

"I see."

"Also, our ship is a little different than most of the others as it has a scattering field which means most other ships can't see us."

"Can I ask why you would have such a ship?"

"Yes, we are a rock band and don't want to bump into any one unexpectedly. The ship is also armed with four pulse cannons just in case we do." said Datch.

"That's a very expensive ship even for a rock band."

"We didn't buy it. It was a gift from our president after we saved his life and fixed Welly Four."

"Yes, we're ambassadors for Welly four as well." added Hagger not wanting to be left out.

"I'm sure you will understand that we need to check you out before allowing her highness on your ship."

"Check away." said Datch.

The bodyguard got out a vid com and scanned them all. The vid com took a while to do the background checks and finally beeped. The bodyguard looked at it and then raised an eyebrow.

"They all check out according to the galactic database." she said.

The other bodyguard turned to the others.

"OK, we will need to scan your ship as well before we'll let her highness on board."

"Sure, no probs. But we have to wait until the security services tell us it's safe."

"Judging by this record, the planet below should be more worried about you setting foot on it. Can I ask you sir, do you make a habit of saving people?"

The Pack all looked at each other and then at Datch who went a little pink.

"Err, it just sort of happens." he said smiling.

"Well, as it looks like the security services are going to take a while, why don't we get some food."

"Her highness does not have food or drinks from bars that have not been vetted."

"She does now." said Rosey pointing to the glass in front of Deena.

"Yes, I do. So what food is good in this bar?"

The two bodyguards looked at each other and then at the Deena.

"Timbo, please could you go and get some menus from the bar." said Datch.

"OK."

Timbo got up and headed across towards the bar, a couple of people spotted him coming and moved well out of the way. He collected the menus and told the barman that they were having food and they would put their hands up when they were ready to order. He turned and headed back to The Packs tables.

The barman looked at a sign behind him that said 'Please order your food at the bar' then back at Timbo and decided this time he would make an exception.

Timbo handed the menus around and they sat looking at them.

"So, what is good?" Deena asked looking at the menu.

"Well, have you had Hacks wings and Weega fries or pizza?" said Carina.

"I've had pizza but not the others."

"What are we thinking folks, hacks and fries all round?"

"Yep, I'm up for that. But I'm still feeling a little full from the last meal, so maybe only a couple of wings." said Hagger.

There was a general consensus that the Hacks and Fries with a side of two pizza's would be good.

"We will abstain from food in case it is drugged with something." said one of the bodyguards.

"You do realise that we have Timbo and therefore, one, it would take a very large amount of drugs to knock him out and two, if the chef tried to drug us, he had better be able to run very fast as when Timbo gets upset you really need to be serval star systems away from him." said Datch and sat back in his seat.

"Yes, and I think you need to chill." added Krissy.

"I couldn't have said it better myself." said Deena.

"Ok, but we will wait until you have eaten first." Said the slightly more relaxed of the bodyguards. Both of them had missed their breakfasts due to the incident.

The food came out and Deena had a bit of everything and decided that hacks wings and fries should be added to the royal menus.

They were on their third round of drinks when the officer who looked after them earlier came walking through the doors. He was carrying a bag in his hands. He spotted them and headed over to them.

He stopped in front of the princess.

"Your highness, we have managed to catch one of the men involved and have found this bag along with a number of others. I believe this is yours."

He gave her the bag.

"Thank you." she said as she opened the bag and looked inside.

"Everything there is in there we think apart from your Jackar" he said.

"NO! not my Jackar." She looked very upset.

"I'm very sorry your highness. We have scanned the arrested man and the other man has left the station with it. We have been trying to track the ship but we believe that it may have been a small private ship which gave a false passenger statement."

"Are you sure he's left?" asked Fred.

"Yes, we were able to get his DNA off of the bag and did a full sweep of the station. There are traces of him going to the docking area and onto a small ship. The ship that we suspect he's on has left the system at interspace seven at which point it was lost from sensors. We're very sorry your highness."

"Did you find out anything else from the other man?" asked one of the bodyguards.

"Yes, he was hired to help get the purse and had been watching you for the last two days. He spotted the Princess out by herself and called the other man. We believe the other man is intending to use the Jackar against the princess in some way as that was the only thing he took."

"It's only used when I get married and I have no plans for that just yet." said Deena.

"Yes, your highness. But it would not look good if the planet found out that you had lost it." said one of the bodyguards.

Deena started to look worried.

"I never thought of it that way." she said.

"Is there anything you can do officer?" asked Tank.

"As the other party has left the system not a lot. We have passed the details of the ship onto the neighbouring star systems but we suspect the ship was running under a false ID."

"So, you don't think anyone will find it?" asked Deena.

"Sorry your highness, but it is highly unlikely."

Deena looked very upset.

"I had thought the security services would find the men and I could just forget about it. This is not good. My dad is going to be very angry with me."

"Yes but at least the security services had captured one of the men."

"I suppose so." she said looking down.

"We will try and get all the information we can for you before you leave."

"Thank you, officer." she said. Her tone was lower now and the bounce had gone from the voice.

"You're welcome your highness. If there is anything else I can do for you please let me know."

"What will happen to the other man?" asked Dapo.

"He will be sentenced and most likely be made to work cleaning the shall we say, more dirty areas of the station."

"I hope he enjoys it." said Datch sarcastically.

"Oh, he won't." said the officer and then he said his goodbyes and left to sort out a cleaning detail for the human waste recycling area of the station.

"Well, I think we can leave folks." said Datch.

"We still need to scan your ship." said one of the bodyguards.

"Clax, could you take err…" Datch looked at the bodyguards hoping for a name. None came. "Her to the ship and we'll follow when it's all done?"

"No probs Datch." he got up.

"Are you coming number 1?"

"Number 1?"

"Yes, until you tell us your name, you are number 1 and she is number 2." He said.

"She is Tate and that is Kato." Said Deena smiling again.

"Ok Tate, follow me."

With that, Clax got up and headed for the door followed by Tate.

After they had gone Deena turned to Kato.

"My dad's going to be mad at me, isn't he?"

"Yes, your highness. I think he is going to be somewhat disappointed in you."

Datch thought for a few moments.

"Maybe we can help. Our ship can do interspace seventeen. I bet we can outrun any small ship. Maybe we can catch him if we get moving. See if the security officer can give us a heading."

"We cannot go putting the Princess in danger." Said Kato.

"We wouldn't, the IPSF upgraded our shields when we helped Arcaneus out. Even five or six bandit ships would have trouble stopping us. Also, all we need to do is track the ship from a distance and then tell the IPSF were to find them."

"And why would the IPSF come if you asked."

"Check my record!" said Datch.

She did and raised another eyebrow.

"OK, so we find them while staying at a safe distance and then call the IPSF to arrest them." said Deena trying to override Kato.

"I'm still not happy about this." Kato said.

"Well, if you think things are getting too risky then you tell us and we back off or get the hell out of there." Said Datch.

"I like it." added Krissy eager to have her first space adventure. That is apart from going into space in the first place, being the first Earthing to go to another planet, sorry, planets and setting up home on an alien world.

"Hmm. And I get to call it off if I'm not happy?" said Kato.

"Yes." said Datch.

"And we will not be putting her highness in danger?"

"No."

"Ok, if we can get the Jackar back it would save a lot of explaining."

They all started smiling and Datch stared grinning.

"I think you should call the officer and ask if he has the heading of the ship, we're after."

"Ok. I'll ask him for it."

# The Passengers

Kato's vid com beeped and Tate appeared on it.

"You're good to bring the Princess down. The ship is safe and checks out ok."

"Thanks." She closed the channel.

"We're good to go. We will swing by our quarters on the way and put our luggage out ready for transport. We are travelling light so we don't have many things. I'll ask for transporter access when we get to your ship if that's ok?"

"Sure, no problem."

They finished their drinks and got up. Kato wanted to go at the front and Timbo went at the back just in case there were any more people that might want to harm the Princess. That way if anyone tried anything they would have to come from the front to stand any chance of surviving let alone succeeding.

They followed Kato down the corridors and into this lift and then that one. It took a good ten minutes to get to the Princess's quarters. They were asked to wait outside and watch the corridor while Kato and Deena went inside to sort out their belongings.

Datch was leaning against the wall looking thoughtful.

"I've been thinking, we haven't had a good adventure for a while have we."

They all turned and looked at him.

"You're going to get the Jackar back for her, aren't you?" said Fred knowing full well what was coming.

"Well, I was thinking it would be nice to have some fun."

"You, can't be thinking of dragging a Princess and her two bodyguards across the stars, are you?" said Peebop.

"Err, well no. I don't think her dad would be happy about that. I thought we could do it while we are having a break."

"So, we chase across the galaxy after a thief before stealing the Jackar back and returning it to the Princess. All in three weeks." said Fred.

"Yes. But we had better do it in two weeks so we have time to party afterwards."

"Hmm, I'm not sure it will be that easy."

"It will be something to do other than sitting on a beach watching the sea wash up and down."

"OK, but only if we get a lead. There is no point doing anything if we don't have one. Also, it's not the sea on Hybaysus, they are just very big lakes."

"Oh, ok."

"Does that mean we're not going to the beach resort?" asked Hagger.

"No, not straight away."

"Oh, I was looking forward to a cold beer."

"You've just had one! Anyway, I'm sure we'll find one on route."

Just then one of the doors opened and Kato came out.

"All sorted?"

"Mine and Tate's things are, I just need to make sure the Princess has her things sorted out."

She turned and went back in the princess's room.

"Maybe we can make another song?" said Dapo who was currently rubbing Tish's shoulder as she had strained it slightly while playing Solar Ball.

"What, about us chasing after a Jackar?"

"Well, I think it should be quite easy to make it work." said Carina.

"Hey, let's try and get it back first before we write a song about it." said Rosey.

Just then the door opened and Kato and Deena came out.

"It's all ready for transport. Shall we go?" said Kato.

"Lead the way. We're parked in bay 97." said Fred.

They followed Kato along to the maze of corridors to the lifts going to the landing bays. They headed up to the landing area and exited the lift into the security check point. After being scanned by the security system, they headed to bay 97.

As they came around the corner into the landing area, the Raven came into view. It was sitting on the pad with its ramp down. The green flames painted on its wings shone brightly in the bays flood lights.

"Wow, that's a nice-looking ship. I love the green flames." said Deena.

"Thanks. If you would like to please follow me." said Datch.

He led the way up the ramp. Tate was standing at the top of it with Clax.

"Welcome to the Raven your highness." Said Clax smiling.

After a quick tour of the ship, Deena was shown to one of the spare rooms. Tate and Kato were given the room next to Deena's.

Kato instructed the transport service to transfer their belongings and after a quick check to make sure everything was there. It was time to leave.

They headed up to the cockpit and found Datch sitting in the pilot's seat going through the pre-flight checks with Clax.

Carina showed Deena to the seat opposite her.

Datch turned to look at everyone.

"Are we ready?" he asked.

Everyone nodded.

"Starlight Control, this is the Raven requesting launch."

"Raven, please put your systems in standby and prepare for lift operation."

"Copy that, Starlight. Putting systems in standby."

Datch's heads up display showed the lift system connected to the landing struts and they had a red box around them showing the ship was still anchored to them. A few moments past and then the comms burst into life again.

"Raven, Lift will engage in fifteen seconds."

There was a shudder as the pad below them started to move upwards. Outside the Raven entered a vertical shaft as the lift systems carried the ship towards the centre of the station.

Datch's heads up display showed him the artificial gravity had engaged and it had also started showing the vectors for the station exit.

The lift started to slow down and the Raven came out of the shaft into a large cylindrical tube with the ends leading into space. All around them were lift shafts heading down to the landing pads. The area was like the inside of a pipe with a rectangular exit at one end and an entrance at the other. The pad below them turned rotating the Raven towards the exit.

Datch could see the other active ships in his display. Some were coming into land while others like the Raven were leaving.

"Raven, Locks will disengage in thirty seconds. Please connect to beacon 34251 for automated station exit."

"Copy that, Starlight. Connecting to beacon."

There was a clunk as the clamps disengaged. The Raven's engines came online and they started to move slowly forwards towards the station exit.

Datch turned and looked at Kato.

"Do you have the vector for the other ship?" he asked.

"Yes, it was heading to the Trident system."

"Starlight control, this is Raven. We will be heading for the Trident system on exit."

"Copy that, Raven. After beacon releases head on vector 364.92,162.54 until you are in clear space."

"Thanks Starlight."

Around them, they could see ships being taken down into the bowels of the station or waiting on their pads, ready for launch. The Raven started to pick up speed, and ahead of them, the exit started to get larger. Flashing lights showed them the way out, but because the ship was on auto, Datch could just sit and watch. The exit looked quite small to start with, but by the time they reached it, it was the size of a city block. The Raven was tiny by comparison. They exited the station and continued to accelerate into space. Two minutes later, the comms burst back into life.

"Raven this is Starlight. Beacon with release in thirty seconds."

Datch place his hands over the controls and waited.

"Raven, you have control."

Datch took the controls and turned the ship onto the new vector. The Raven continued to accelerate away from the station, heading out into the darkness of space. Another five minutes passed, and then the comms burst into life again.

"Raven, this is Starlight control. You are now clear to navigate. Have a safe trip."

"Thanks Starlight. Raven out."

"Raven, set course for the Trident system, interspace twelve."

"Course laid in Journey time 72.4 hours. Do you wish standard alarm?"

"Yes please. Engage."

"Interspace Twelve?" asked Clax.

"Yes, we don't want to overtake the other ship without seeing it, do we?"

"True."

The ship turned to right and then the stars outside vanished for a moment before starting to flicker.

"Kato, did you get the ships ID?"

"Yes, It's AYHG19237394HGXXX47P75."

"Raven, can you keep scanning for a ship with that ID please and alert us if it's detected."

"Commencing search for AYHG19237394HGXXX47P75. Alarm will be triggered on detection of ID."

Datch stopped and thought for a moment and then added.

"Raven on detection engage the scattering field."

"Scattering field will engage on detection."

"OK folks, Let's go and chill for a bit. I feel like a game of Solar Ball." Datch said getting up.

"I'm up for that." Said Tish.

"I'm not very good but would you mind if I played?" said Deena.

"Sure, the more the merrier." said Carina.

They headed down to the cargo bay and started playing.

As the hours passed, Kato and Tate started to relax a bit. After a while, they even started to join in with the Solar Ball. After Solar Ball, the party ended up chilling in the rec room and watching a movie. By the time evening came, they had stopped being bodyguards and were more normal. They still insisted on calling Deena "Your Highness," but they were now a lot more relaxed.

Datch got up from the sofa and headed to the door.

"I'm going to check on the systems."

He left and went up to the cockpit and sat down.

"Raven, display tactical plot please and show ship ID's."

The holo projectors came on and started to display stars in front of him. Then ships started to appear in the display with little boxes above them showing their name and heading.

Datch sat and watched as the space for twenty lightyears around them slowly appeared in the cockpit.

'Where are you?' he thought looking at the ships traveling across the cockpit.

Just then Kato came walking into the cockpit. She stopped and turned to Datch.

"I just wanted to say thank you for all you are doing."

"You're welcome. Please sit down."

He gestured to the co-pilots seat.

"Thank you." she said sitting down.

"I hope you are enjoying the trip?"

"To be honest, it is much safer transporting the Princess this way. The liner would have been a nightmare from a security standpoint. So, yes, much better. What are you doing?"

"I was just looking for the other ship. This is the ship's tactical plot. It's showing twenty light years around the ship. I was hoping something would show up by now."

"This is a very advanced display for a ship this size." she said looking at the ships.

"As we said, it's a little bit special. It was a pirate ship before we were given it and then the IPSF made a few adjustments for us. She can do interspace seventeen and has an extra twenty tera watts of the shielding. The Raven is a tough little ship."

"So, what are you thinking?"

"Well, If I can spot the ship, we can follow it and see where it goes."

"What then?"

"Well, we can ask the authorities to hold him and we can get Deena's Jackar back."

"It's a nice plan but some star systems may not be happy to do that. The theft took place of Starlight after all."

"I know but hopefully they will if we explain about Deena."

"Hopefully."

They sat back watching the holo display for a while until Carina stuck her head in the cockpit.

"Are you two going to be sitting there all night?" she said.

"Oh, sorry babes. It was sort of mesmerising. What's happening?"

"We're going to start another movie and this time we have some movie food to go with it."

"Ok, let's leave the computer to it."

They got up and followed Carina back to the rec room.


The next day came and went with nothing out of the ordinary on the tactical plot. They were following the same ships, all headed to the Trident system, and nothing was out of place. They passed the time with Solar Ball, a racing game, and some more films.


It wasn't the same as being on a liner, but the Princess was really enjoying it. She could just be herself and didn't have to be followed around everywhere. That said, there wasn't really anywhere to go on a ship the size of the Raven.

Kato and Tate were also enjoying the trip, as they didn't have anything to do and could relax.

It was just after they had finished eating their evening meal when the ship's alarm went off. Datch, Clax, and Kato headed up to the cockpit. The tactical alert was flashing.

Datch sat down and pressed a couple of buttons.

"Raven, what is the tactical alert?"

"A ship with the ID has been detected after the craft had changed heading."

"Show me."

The tactical plot appeared in front of them and then started to display the ships around them. A ship was displayed with a red circle around it. It was about ten light years away and displaying an ID number different to the one they were looking for.

"Raven, why is the ID number different?"

"The ship in question cycled through a number of ID's four light years ago including the one you asked me to scan for. It has now changed to the current ID displayed but scans have confirmed the ship's identity."

"It changed its ID number. Wow." said Clax looking at it.

After a few moments the ship changed its heading and started moving away on a different vector. Then after a few moments it's ID changed back to the one they were looking for.

"You can say that again. Raven, what is the ships new heading?" asked Datch.

"The ship is now on a vector for the Tray star system."

"What is in Tray system?"

"The Tray system consists of five planets and two large asteroid fields. None of the planets can support life and are uninhabited. However, there are a number of space stations and mining outposts on the planets, as the system does have a high level of rare elements. Warning: There are no IPSF outposts in the system, and the area has been linked to a number of pirate attacks. Accessing the system is not advised."

"Well, that explains why he's going there." Said Clax.

"We can't take the Princess there. It would be far too dangerous." said Kato looking concerned.

"Yes, I think your right." said Datch.

Just then Carina came in with Tate and Fred.

"What's up?" said Fred.

"We found the ship. It was running under a false ID and just changed its course to head for a lawless star system. The Raven only spotted it because it switched its ID." said Datch.

"Are we going after it?" asked Carina.

"No, it's too risky with Deena on board." Said Kato.

"What is?" said Deena walking up behind the rest of them.

"The Tray system. The ship we were looking for just headed that way."

"Oh. can't we follow it?"

"NO, your highness. Tate and I would probably get executed twice for taking you in there and your dad would likely make sure it hurt a lot."

"So, we can't get my Jackar back?"

"Not that way. It looks like we're going to have to tell your farther what has happened."

"You will both get in trouble for letting me out of your sight."

"We know, but there is no way I'm letting you go to that system. The pirates would love to get their hands on a prize like you. You would fetch a huge ransom for them."

"My dad would send ships to get me back."

"And all they would find would be your body. No is no, your highness."

"She's right Deena. We can't take you there." said Carina.

Deena looked really upset. It was very rare that people would say no to her and now a lot of people doing it all at the same time.

"Maybe your dad will send ships to get your Jackar back?" said Rosey.

"I wouldn't think so. The chances of success would be very slim. The pirates would see them coming and go to ground destroying the Jackar in the process."

"Well, at least we can tell him where they are."

"I think we should drop you off on your home world before heading to our resort."

"That's very kind of you."

"It's only twenty light years difference and we can get the Raven refuelled while we're there."

"Thank you."

"Raven, set course for the Thoth star system interspace seventeen with standard Alarm. Also, shutdown tactical systems." said Datch.

"Course laid in. Journey time will be twelve hours thirty-two minutes."

"Engage."

The stars outside stopped flickering and the Raven slowly turned in space facing towards another star system before the stars winked out and started to flicker again.

"Let's go and get a beer. I think it's going to be a long twelve hours." said Fred.

They got up and headed back to the rec room where they picked up some drinks before heading to the cargo bay for a bit of stress relief.

# Thoth

The next morning after breakfast, there was a strange atmosphere in the Raven. Everyone could tell that the Princess was worried. The two bodyguards were also getting concerned about the day ahead of them. Everyone else felt like they were walking on eggshells.

Datch and Clax headed to the cockpit and sat down. They were still a few light-years out, but at interspace seventeen, it wouldn't be long before the alarm went off.

"What's the plan then?" asked Clax while looking out the window.

"Land, head to a bar while the ship is refuelled and then leave. I can't see us having a party this time."

"No, that's true. That's not what I meant though."

"You mean are we going chasing after the Jackar?"

"Yes."

"I don't know. I want to help the Princess but I'm not sure we can. The Tray system doesn't look that friendly."

"True."

They sat looking at the stars as they flickered past.

"It will be nice to have a boring break for a change." said Clax with a smirk on his face.

"Hmm…"

"But I don't think we are going to though."

Datch looked across at Clax. He knew him better than anyone.

"Well, let's see." said Datch smiling.

"Yes, let's see." said Clax with a grin.

The arrival alarm went off and everyone started to appear in the cockpit. After everyone had sat down Datch picked up his headset and put it on.

"Thoth control. This is the starship Raven on approach to Thoth four. Please be advised that we have Princess Deena with us along with her bodyguards."

"Raven, please repeat."

Datch did and there were a few moments silence before a different voice came on the comms.

"Raven, please ask the Princess to transmit her ID and the Bodyguards to transmit theirs."

"They need your ID's folks." Said Datch turning around.

"Datch, can you give me a direct link please." said Kato.

Datch press a few buttons.

"There, you should have an open channel."

The was a burst of static from the comms system.

"Raven, IDs confirmed. Please wait while I transfer you to imperial command."

The comms made a small hiss and then burst back into life.

"Good morning, Raven. Please lock on to beacon 1 for the Palace landing area. You will be on pad seven. Automated landing is mandatory for this landing area."

"Locking on to the beacon. The Raven is yours Thoth control."

"Thank you, Raven. Please note though, you are now under control of imperial command and will not be following standard flight paths. Do not attempt to change course."

Datch turned to look at Kato. She just nodded.

"Understood Thoth control."

The Raven approached the planet and dropped out of interspace right in the middle of a fleet of military ships. They were not big but you wouldn't want to upset them. Five of them broke off from the main group and formed up around the Raven.

"This is normal." said Kato, "They are just our royal escort down."

The Raven dropped down through the atmosphere with the other ships in formation around them. In the distance a city could be seen with glittering towers and a lattice of transport tubes running above the streets. On the right side was a large building set in perfectly landscaped gardens. At its edge was a landing area with a large perimeter fence surrounding it. The Raven started to slow down and drop towards the surface.

"That's the Palace over there." said Deena pointing at the building.

"Nice looking place." Said Clax.

Just then the comms burst into life.

"Raven, landing control will be ready in 30 seconds."

"Thank you, Command."

Datch put his hands over the controls and got ready.

"Raven, you have control. Please wait after landing for a reception party to come to your ship."

"Copy that command."

Datch moved the Raven across the landing area to pad seven and then slowly dropped her on to it.

"Command, Raven has landed."

"Reception will be with you in two minutes. Command out."

Datch turned to the others,

"Well Deena, you're home."

"OK, Thanks, I had better talk to my dad and explain why I've come home with you."

"OK."

"Kato, can you sort out the luggage please?"

"Yes, your highness."

She turned to The Pack.

"I have messaged a head and you are all expected at the palace."

"Err... we don't have our posh clothes on." Said Rosey.

"I'm sure his majesty will understand as this is a bit short notice."

They all got up and headed to the cargo bay stopping to get Deena's, Tate's and Kato's things on route. Datch dropped the ramp and they waited for the reception party to arrive.

A few moments later a number of vehicles pull up behind the Raven and a number of guards got out forming a corridor to the bottom of the ramp.

"Ok, we can go now." said Kato.

Deena walked down the ramp, followed by Kato and Tate. The Pack followed behind.

The guards all saluted as the princess walked past. A man standing next to the lead vehicle opened the rear door. The princess walked over to the door, and the man bowed. She got into the vehicle, followed by Kato and Tate.

The Pack were shown to the vehicles behind. Once everyone was seated, the motorcade set off in the direction of the palace.

The vehicles passed lakes with fountains and beautiful hedges that had been cut into various artistic shapes. The lawns were mowed so perfectly that they looked like carpets, and there was a complex network of paths linking the different areas. As they drew closer to the palace, they could see all the intricate stonework and ornate stone carvings that were dotted all the way around the structure. Large glass windows and doors filled the spaces in between the walls.

The motorcade arrived at the palace and pulled up outside two huge doors with five marble pillars on each side. The Princess got out of the first vehicle and headed up the steps, followed by Kato and Tate. The Pack got out of their vehicle and were led up the steps and through the doors by an aide.

Inside, there was a large corridor lined with marble pillars and arches. The pillars and arches were all decorated with fancy carvings and gilded edges. The carpet was red and gold with a very thick pile, and it had a little gold crown pattern in it.

The Pack were taken into a large side room full of paintings and antique furniture. The member of staff turned to them and said,

"Please, wait here and his majesty the king will send for you shortly. Would you like any refreshments while you are waiting?"

"We're OK at the moment, thank you." said Datch.

They made themselves comfy and waited to be called.

"It's a nice place they have here." said Clax looking at some of the paintings that were hanging on the walls.

"Yes, I like the one with the naked woman on it." said Hagger trying sound intelligent.

"You would." said Rosey and gave him a hard stare.

"No, I meant artistically speaking."

"Yes, right." The stare carried on.

Hagger started looking at the various antiques around the room as that seemed to be a safer bet and narrowly avoided fondling a carving of a naked woman on the back of a chair.

"It's a shame we couldn't get the Jackar back." said Tish.

"I know. But at least we have got the Princess home safe and sound." said Clax.

"Yes." said Datch looking into space for a moment.

About thirty minutes later, a member of staff came to fetch them. They were taken through the palace to a large room with a very large desk at the far end. Deena was standing next to it with Kato. In front of the desk was a tall man dressed in a suit.

A man next to the door said in a loud voice.

"Ladies and Gentlemen, His royal highness King Janfar of Thoth."

The Pack approached him and then all bowed.

"Good morning, all. I must apologise but normally someone would announce you all. Please could you introduce yourselves."

"Hello, your majesty. I am Datch and this is Carina..." Datch went around everyone introducing them.

Afterwards the King looked at them all.

"I would like to personally thank you all for helping my daughter. If you had not been there, I don't know what would have happened."

"It was nothing your majesty. We just came across her in need of help and frightened the attackers off." said Datch.

"Well, thank you. My daughter and I are very grateful. I would love to talk to you more, but unfortunately, I'm in the middle of trade talks at the moment. I did however want to thank you personally for what you have done. If there is anything we can help you with while you're here, please don't hesitate to ask."

"Thank you, your majesty. We are not stopping long as we have a reservation a few light years away. But if you know a good bar where we can get some food and a drink while our ship is refuelled that would be great."

"Hmm. Well, I don't get out much but my aid over there will be able to point you in the right direction."

"Thank you, your majesty."

"Thank you again and now you must excuse me as I have matters to attend to."

They all bowed again and the King left the room followed by Deena and Kato.

The Pack were shown out. As they left, the aid told them about a bar on the first city stop from the spaceport. The motorcade took them back through the gardens to the Raven.

Datch sat down in the cockpit and put on his headset.

"Command, this is the Raven requesting clearance to fly to the spaceport service area."

"Raven, please bring your systems to standby and we will clear you a flight path."

There was a short pause.

"Raven, cleared for launch. Head on vector 223,23.6 you are cleared for landing on pad twenty-seven."

"Copy that command and thank you."

"You're welcome, Raven. Enjoy the city."

Datch piloted the Raven the short distance to the spaceport. The flight path took them over the city, and the whole trip lasted only five minutes. The city itself was similar in size and shape to Yuland City on Bellatrix Five. The layout was a bit different, as the spaceport was on the west side, opposite the palace. It had large parks surrounding it, as well as a boating lake and a number of small, wooded areas. The city's main retail area was in the centre, and the industrial area was in the north. However, it was mostly light industry, and there was not much of it. The rest of the city was mostly housing, with an occasional retail park dotted here and there.

Datch landed in the spaceports service area and they all headed off to the cargo bay.

As they exited the Raven, a droid was waiting at the bottom of the ramp. Datch sorted out the refuelling with it and asked for directions to exit into the city.

"Ok, folks let's go find a bar." said Datch.

They found their way out of the spaceport and to the high-speed transit line that ran into the city centre. The Pack entered one of the transit tube carriages, and it started to move off. It only took a few moments to cross the park and arrive at the first stop on the city side, where the aid had suggested they get off.

They spotted the bar they had been told about. It was just a short walk down the road and bordered the park. The building was a large two-story structure with creamy white walls.

Outside of it was a seating area on a large grass lawn. There were a number of tables and chairs, and some larger benches at one side, all of which had parasols over them to keep the sun off.

The Pack headed to the benches and sat down. A few moments later, a waiter came walking over.

"Good afternoon, ladies and gentlemen. How may I help you?"

"We're after a few drinks and something to eat while our ship is refuelled." said Fred.

"OK, I will take your drinks orders first and bring the menus out with them if that is ok, sir?"

"Sure, we would like eight large beers, two of which alcohol free, three glasses of white wine and a large Old Man's Boots with Grucks please."

"We do not have Old Man's Boots," He paused for a moment looking into space before continuing, "But we have some Royal Spirit that is very similar?"

Fred looked at Hagger who nodded.

"Yes, that will be fine thanks." he said.

"Thank you. I shall return shortly with your drinks."

With that the waiter headed inside.

"So, what's the plan then?" asked Clax.

"Well, they said it was going to take seven hours to refuel the Raven. So, I suppose we just chill here. Then it's a quick six-hour trip from here to Hybaysus six at interspace seventeen and then the resort complex." said Datch.

"I can't wait to get in the sea. I really fancy a swim after being cooped up in the Raven for ten days straight." said Rosey.

"I agree. It's a bit small for that length of time." added Tish.

"I'm loving it." said Krissy, who had seen more planets in the last two months than she had ever dreamed of existing.

Earth was now almost a distant memory. A small blue world where her life had begun. Now the stars were her playground, with thousands of new worlds to explore. The galaxy was living up to everything that Datch and Carina had told her when she left Earth.

The waiter came back with the drinks and handed out a number of menus. After a few minutes of debate, the food was ordered: salads, fish dinners, a couple of pasta dishes, and a cheeseburger for Hagger, who thought healthy food was unhealthy.

The Pack spent the next couple of hours debating the monarchy versus the presidential structure back on Bellatrix. The afternoon went by and turned into early evening.

The Pack were making the most of the fresh air and were just watching a cargo ship come into land at the spaceport when Kato and Tate came walking over to them.

"Hello again." said Datch looking to see if Deena was behind them.

"Hello. We thought we may find here."

"Where's Deena?"

"Err… We are no longer in charge of her."

"Oh…"

"Yes. The King was not happy that we let her out of our sight. So, we've been suspended."

"That's a bummer. So, what are you going to do now?"

"We're going to go after the pirates who took the Jackar. If we get it back maybe the king will let us have our jobs back."

"So, what can we do for you?" asked Fred.

"We're hoping you can give us all the information you collected from scanning the ship that they were using, including the registry numbers."

"Hmm… Yes, I can give you a copy of the data when we get back to the Raven." said Datch.

"You know it's going to be hard to find them without a ship?" said Fred.

"Yes, but we know what system they are in so we'll get passage there as miners. When we're there, we just have to find the ship and watch for them coming or going."

"Yes, and then we have a little chat with them." said Tate grinning.

"That sounds very easy." said Fred.

"I don't think it will be that simple but that's the plan."

"Well, we're going to head back in a couple of hours. The spaceport was quite busy and had a six hour wait for servicing." said Datch.

"OK, do you mind if we wait with you?"

"Sure, pull up a chair."

Tate and Kato sat down and ordered some drinks. As they talked, Datch watched them from across the table. They were not bodyguards anymore but just two people trying to get stolen property back. The two hours soon went by and it was almost time to head back to the Raven when Kato and Tate went to the bathroom. Datch turned to the others.

"Guy's, why don't we help them?" he asked.

"Why?" said Fred.

"Well, it will be a bit of an adventure and fun."

"I don't think heading to an almost lawless mining outpost will be fun but I like how you're thinking." Said Clax.

"Hmm… Well, it may be interesting. Not as dangerous as helping save Arcaneus." Added Dapo.

"Well. I think we should." said Krissy who was now thinking that it would be exciting.

"Do we get an after party?" asked Hagger.

"An after party? We're not saving a planet or any presidents, just a Jackar." said Tank.

"I would think there maybe a few beers in it though." said Dapo.

"So, are we all in?" asked Datch.

They all nodded one after another.

"Ok, we'll that's a go then."

Timbo started to look into space.

"Why do I get the feeling that we're going to have a load more cargo when we get back to the Raven." said Fred looking across at Timbo.

Datch looked over at him.

"Timbo, don't forget the beer." he said.

"Already on the list." he said still starring into space.

"What's he doing?" asked Krissy.

"Ordering supplies with his implant." said Carina.

"I should have realised; I'm still getting use to mine."

"It takes time. It took me nearly two years before I stopped thinking about it and just did it." said Tish.

Just then Kato and Tate came walking back.

"So, we going to head back?" said Kato.

"Err, we're not quite ready. Timbo eta?"

"About an hour."

"Cool."

"Err, an hour. We were hoping to get going." said Tate.

"That's not a problem. We're just waiting for supplies." said Dapo.

"Err, can't you wait at the ship?"

"Well, that would be ok apart from the fact we're coming with you."

"What! This is not a trip into a friendly bar or two. These people will not be very friendly." said Tate raising her voice.

Datch looked at Kato.

"You haven't told her, have you?"

"No, there was no need. Only I have seen your security information." She turned to Tate, "These folks are more than able to handle themselves. Trust me."

"Right!" said Datch, "Time to come up with a plan."

They sat talking and scheming for the next hour before heading to the Raven.

The spaceport was very busy with ships coming and going. The Raven sat waiting for them in the service yard. A member of staff came over to them and as they approached the ship.

"Good evening." he said walking up them.

"Good evening, is everything OK?"

"Yes sir. The cargo has been loaded and the ship is fully refuelled. If I can just ask you to approve payment."

"Sure." Datch looked at the man's Vid com and it beeped.

"I've added a ten-credit tip for you as well."

"Thank you, sir."

They went up the ramp and into the Raven. In the centre of the cargo bay was a large pile of crates and a stack of cans of beer. Timbo, Tank and Peebop stopped and started sorting it out and putting it away in the process.

Datch headed to the cockpit with Clax and sat down. They started going through the pre-flight checks while the others sorted themselves out. By the time they had finished everyone one had sat down. Datch picked up his headset and put it on.

"Everyone ready?" he asked looking around.

Everyone nodded in agreement.

"Ok then. Let's get this show on the road!"

He turned to face the front.

"Taliss Control – This is the Raven ready for departure to the Geldamore star system."

"Raven, you are number six in the que. Please bring your systems online and hover at twenty metres."

"Taliss Control, copy that."

Datch brought the systems online and lifted off.

The Raven hung in the air waiting for clearance. Around it ships were coming into land and others were taking off.

"Raven, please lock on to beacon 172. Thirty seconds until your launch."

Datch pressed a few virtual buttons.

"Thanks Control. Locked on."

"Raven, Launch when green."

Datch turned the Raven to face the beacon and waited. A few seconds later, the beacon turned green in his heads-up display. He increased thrust and fell in behind a freighter, following it into the sky. The shipping lanes were very busy, and Datch was having to really concentrate. He would have asked for automated launch, but he had been too busy thinking about the trip.

The sky darkened to a deep, velvety black as the Raven reached orbit. The beacon in his heads-up display flashed to the right, signalling clear space. Datch's heart raced as he increased power, sending the ship hurtling into the void.

"Thoth control, Raven is clear."

"Have a safe trip, Raven. Control out."

"Raven, set course for the Tray system, interspace sixteen. Normal Alarm and turn on scattering field one hour before arrival."

"Warning! The Tray system is not a governed star system. Privateers and other felons will be present."

"We know. Engage!"

The stars winked out and started to flicker.

"Journey time will be eighteen hours."

"Raven, when the scattering field is turned on start scanning for the ship we scanned for on the way to Thoth."

"Scanning will commence one hour from Tray system."

"Ok, let's go get a beer" said Datch getting up.

"Yes, and carry on talking about what we're going to do when we get there!" added Fred.

They headed to the rec room and, after they had all gotten a beer and sat down, Datch turned on the vid screen.

"Raven, please display the Tray system using the holo emitters and show all outposts along with outpost data," he asked.

The Tray system appeared on the vid and then expanded out across the room. The star moved to the centre of the room, and the planets moved to their positions before several asteroid belts appeared. The outposts had small boxes next to them stating their population, tech level, and services.

"Well, I don't think they would be going to a mining outpost," said Clax after inspecting some of the outposts.

"They're not trying to hide. They don't know we're on to them."

"True, there would be no point," said Kato. "It would have to be a population centre that has interspace data links so they could sell the Jackar."

"Raven, only show the large population centres with access to the interspace network." said Datch.

A lot of the floating lights vanished, leaving three. One was on a planetoid, and the other two were on large asteroids. Datch looked closely at them. The ones on the asteroids were mostly mineral processing plants with no more than a large town's population, but the planetoid had a small city on it.

"Well, I think we should head to the city complex," said Datch after a few moments' thought.

"Why?" asked Tate.

"Well, one, they could hide easily if anyone came looking for them," said Datch. "Two, it would have access to coms links that they needed to sell the Jackar. And three, there are a lot of places to spend money."

"Why would they want to spend money?" asked Fred.

"They're criminals," replied Datch with a grin.

"Yes, criminals like to drink a lot," added Hagger.

He couldn't argue with that logic.

"Okay, so we go to the city," said Fred.

"Yes, and then we'll look for the ship. If it's there, the Raven will spot it."

"What if it's not?" said Fred.

"Then we wait for it."

"And what if it still doesn't come?"

"Hmm… Well, after two weeks, we'll have to give up, as we need to get ready for the next gig on the tour."

"Sounds like a plan," said Peebop.

"Say we find them, then what?" asked Fred.

"We will have a little talk to them," said Kato with an evil grin on her face.

"Okay. We'll leave that bit up to you," said Rosey, not liking the look on Kato's face.

They all sat back and started to relax with a drink.

Next morning, the Pack sat having breakfast when Kato and Tate walked in.

"Morning." Said Datch as they came and sat down.

"Morning all."

Carina sorted breakfast for them and after they had eaten it, Kato turned to them.

"I've had a message from the Princess. She says they want a hundred million credits and the King to abdicate."

"Wow, that's a lot of credits." said Hagger eating some toast.

"Yes, but why the king bit?" asked Datch.

"I don't know, I suspect the king must have had a run in with them in the past. He has been known for clamping down on pirate activity." said Kato.

"Oh, sort of payback then."

"I take it the king won't do it, though?" asked Carina.

"I doubt it. The loss of his daughter's Jackar will be very embarrassing for him and will damage some of his support on the planet. But it would be highly unlikely to cause the collapse of the monarchy."

"Hmm… so what else did Deena say?" asked Datch.

"She said that the note was printed out on a local print system and was delivered by hand to the palace. They went to check the print system out and found that the file had deleted itself using some sort of virus."

"Anything else?"

"The thief said to have the credits ready for dispatch next week using data packs stored on data cubes. Also, the King must address the population before the next contact."

"That's clever, they can get the credits without anyone being able to trace them," added Fred.

"What, not at all?" asked Rosey.

"No, the data packets are credits, it would be like someone handing you a coin and then it vanishes and your account getting bigger. If it's done at Tray for instance there would be no way to trace them."

"So, I still don't understand why they want the King to abdicate. It would not serve any purpose."

"Well, he won't."

They finished their breakfast and sat drinking a coffee.

About an hour later the ships alarm went off and they headed up to the cockpit.

# Tray

The tactical system was displaying the Tray system and showing all the ships currently in flight. None of which were displaying the correct ID code.

Datch sat in his seat and pressed a few buttons.

"It doesn't look like they have a central flight control for the system. Just local ones for landing and docking procedures. Raven, please scan for landing frequencies at the city on the planetoid closest to the star."

"Communication frequencies found. Do you wish to open a link?"

"Not at the moment. Just keep scanning for the ship's ID and change course for the planetoid."

"Course correction made."

Kato turned to Datch.

"Err… no disrespect but you're going to stick out like a sore thumb in there. A lot of the population of this system are lowlifes and look like they've been through the mill a few times."

Datch looked at her for a moment, and then looked at the others. They did look like a bunch of well-to-do folks.

"Carina, do we still have that gear we had for that horror festival?"

She looked thoughtful for a moment.

"Yes, it's in the storage room at the back. Why?"

"Let's make us look badass!" said Datch with a grin.

"I like you're thinking." said Tank.

"Clax, I think you, Tank, Peebop and Fred should stay on the ship. You can watch for trouble that way and if we need to get out of here in a hurry, you'll be able to have the Raven ready."

"Err… And who is going to look after you?" asked Fred.

"We'll have Timbo, Kato and Tate."

There was no doubting that the three of them would be more than a match for most felons.

"Ok, I'll get the makeup." Said Carina.

She got up and headed to the storeroom. Two minutes later, she was back with a big makeup box.

"Datch, you're first. What were you thinking?"

"Well, I would like a nice scar down one side of my face and give me a black eye so I look like I've been fighting."

"Okay. Come to my seat where I can work on you easier."

Carina set to work transforming Datch. It took about fifteen minutes, and then Datch turned to Kato.

"Well, do I look rough enough?" he asked.

Kato was quite surprised. It looked very real, and in a dimly lit bar, no one would know it was fake.

"Err… Yes, in fact, very good."

"Cool."

Datch went back and sat in his seat.

One by one, the exploration party was transformed into a bunch of rough mining types. Even the girls, who were normally very fashion conscious, looked like they could handle themselves in a bar fight.

Ahead of them was the star Tray, a brown dwarf that gave off a tiny amount of light compared to Bellatrix. The planetoid with the city on it was in a very close orbit with the star, and because of that, they were going to be getting very close to the star itself. The star was slowly dying and only had a few million years left after which it would run out of fuel and turn dark and cold. Datch scanned the system for the ship, but there was still no sign of any of its ID codes.

The Raven started to near the star. They were so close that you could see the lines of nuclear force running across its surface. The shields flashed as charged particles hit them on their way across space. Then the planetoid appeared in front of them. It was more like a moon than a planet, with a protective dome covering a small city in one of the craters. Around the outside were ore processing facilities and large solar farms, turning the sun's small amount of energy into the power for the city and the factories within. Towards the crater rim was the docking tunnel.

"Raven, turn off the scattering field." said Datch.

"The field has been deactivated."

Datch opened the comms.

"Tray 1, this the Raven requesting landing instructions."

There was a pause and then.

"Raven, please state the nature of your visit?"

"Tray 1, We are here on business with one of the mining companies."

"Thank you, Raven. You're cleared for approached. Landing bay thirty-one."

"Copy that Tray 1. On approach."

Datch headed for the crater. There was no law out here, just a small security force paid for by the mining companies, and they were only interested in keeping their goods safe.

Datch dropped down into the crater and entered the docking tunnel. It was a long, clear tube heading down the crater wall and into the dome with the city in it. Every hundred metres, there was a circle of lights lighting the way down the shaft.

As the Raven flew inside it, they went through a number of forcefields, and each time the ship would slow down.

"What are the forcefields for?" asked Dapo.

"They're for atmosphere management," said Clax. "As we pass through each one, the atmosphere gets thicker. Looks like there's just one more to go."

Datch was keeping the Raven almost in the centre of the tube. At the end of the tube was one more forcefield. As the Raven passed through it, the tube opened out into the dome, and there in front of them was the landing area. There were quite a lot of large bays, and most of them were full of cargo ships ready to take the processed ore to the more populated areas of the galaxy. Then, on the right, was a landing area for smaller ships.

Datch spotted bay 31. It was very basic, and had a ramp leading up the side to the main street. There were no security checkpoints, no immigration control, only a gate at the top to act as a barrier from the road and the rest of the city.

Datch brought the Raven in for a soft landing and shut down the flight systems.

"OK folks, we're here. Clax if you keep an eye on the tactical plot for the ship. If you see it, contact me on my vid com. Remember folks, this rock only has about a third of normal gravity so don't go jumping about." He said as he got up.

"You be careful out there." said Fred.

"Don't worry, I'm taking my pistol just in case." said Datch.

"I'll grab mine too." said Carina.

"When did you two get pistols? I thought you got rifles on your honeymoon." said Rosey.

"We did, but we got pistols as well in case something snuck up on us in the jungle."

Kato looked at them. Anyone else would have taken vids and fly repellent, but not these folks. She was starting to realize why they were able to take on entire planets.

"Timbo, you got your gear?"

"Yes, Datch. Everything apart from the pulse cannon I wanted. I tried to buy one on Thoth, but they wanted to know what ship it was going to be put on. When I told them I wanted to carry it, they laughed and wouldn't give it to me."

Tate raised her eyebrow.

"OK then, well, I'm sure we won't need it in the bars." said Datch.

They all headed down to the cargo bay.

Kato stopped next to the cargo bay door and turned to look at Datch.

"OK, before we go out just let me and Tate take the lead. We had better split up but it will be up to you to watch our backs. If you and Carina come with me, Rosey and Hagger go with Tate and Tish, Dapo and Krissy follow along behind with Timbo."

They all nodded, and Timbo went over to the corner and picked up a large bag.

"Err... Timbo, what's in the bag?"

"My anti-aircraft missile system. They sold me that!" He grinned a very wide grin, which would have made most people turn and run for the hills in fear.

"You know we're going in a bar or two, don't you?" said Datch.

"Yes, but we're hunting a ship."

"Timbo, it won't be in the bar."

"It might be outside, though."

"In the street?"

"It might be, or hovering above it."

Datch gave up.

"Just try not to blow a hole in the dome, ok?"

"OK."

Kato was starting to worry that they wouldn't find the Jackar due to it being blown up along with the person who had got it. She had visions of a pair of smoking boots in her head and a very big hole in the atmosphere where the person had been standing.

"Err, please can you try not to blow up the person with the anti-aircraft missile system? It would destroy the Jackar as well as them." She couldn't believe she just said that.

"OK. Are we ready?" said Datch.

There was another round of nodding.

"Right, we'll go first. Give us a couple of minutes then Tate you come and finally you guys. We'll meet up outside the first bar we come to." Said Kato.

With that Datch, Carina and Kato left the ship and headed down the ramp and into the town.

The town smelled of heavy machinery fumes, junk food, and smoke. The air was breathable, but you wouldn't want to live there for too long. The buildings were all on top of each other, and the streets were quite narrow, making the whole place seem claustrophobic. It looked like the construction companies had just put buildings on top of other buildings without thinking about how they connected together. They overlapped at odd angles, and the power and comms connections were hanging out of them like some deranged spider had gone on a webbing rampage. To add to the mix, most things had been painted various shades of black to absorb as much energy from the star as possible.

They walked down the street, heading towards the centre. On either side were large warehouses belonging to shipping companies and wholesalers dealing in ore of one sort or another. Each of them had very large security guards on the doors, all of whom were armed. As they continued down the street, the warehouses gave way to a couple of hotels and then a bar. The bar itself appeared to have an apartment complex built over the top of it, rather than being part of it.

"Let's try in here."

They walked inside and crossed over to the bar.

Kato looked around. The place had an eating area with some diners enjoying their meals and a vid next to the bar displaying stocks and share prices.

They arrived at the bar and waited for the barman to come over.

The officer on the starlight station had given Kato the images from the security systems on the station before they left and she had copied it to her vid com.

When the barman walked over, she asked him if he had seen the man. The barman shook his head.

"We don't let that sort of being in here mam." he said looking hard at Datch.

"Ok, Thanks."

They left the bar and stood outside next to the door waiting for the others to turn up. Tate came up the street with Rosey and Hagger. They stood looking at the menu next to the door pretending to read it. Kato move near to Tate.

"If you three go down that street over there, turn right and follow it down. Then, turn right again. We'll meet up at the bar at the bottom of the street."

"Ok, if we find him, I'll call you on ship coms."

Kato went back to Datch and Carina.

Tate, Rosey and Hagger walked off down the street to the left. Leaving the three of them standing in the street. Then it was Timbo, Tish, Dapo and Krissy's turn. They were given the centre street and then Kato, Datch and Carina took off down the one to the right.

The road Datch went down was a lot busier with people and aliens milling about, and there were a couple more bars a bit further down. One had some tables outside and the smell of exotic scents wafted out, masking the smells of the city. The other had neon lighting outside, but part of it was broken.

They went into the one with the scents and found that it was an alien bar. After some very strange looks, they left and headed to the one with the broken sign outside.

"Can we get a drink in here? The air is starting to make my throat dry." said Carina.

"OK, I'll message the others and let them know we're in the," He stared at the sign above the door, "'Last Chance'. Wow, what a name."

He took out his Vid com and messaged the other groups.

They walked through the door. The inside was dimly lit, with very basic furniture, some of which looked like it had seen a bar fight or two. There were a few extra bits of leg taped together where they had been damaged in the fights. There was a raised area that divided the room into two sections. These seemed to be very rough or extremely rough. The bar itself was lit up with neon lights and had a number of fridge units behind it, all with security locks on to stop anyone taking things during the regular fights. They looked around and spotted a number of tables at the back of the room in the raised section that were almost in darkness due to only half of the lights working.

Kato turned to Datch.

"Let's go over there. We can watch the bar without being seen. I'll go get the drinks. I take it beers are, ok?" she asked.

Datch looked at the bar. There didn't seem to be much else to drink and the guys sitting at the end of the bar had vapor coming of his drink.

"Sure, as long as they are not smoking."

"Ok. Just check the seats before you sit down in case someone died underneath them." Added Kato.

Datch and Carina went to the seats while Kato approached the bar.

"What are you having?" asked the barman.

"Three beers please."

"Sure, coming right up. I haven't seen you before. Are you new in town?"

He started pulling the drinks.

"Yes, we're just here on business. You haven't seen this man, have you? We're meant to be meeting him here for a business deal." She held up a picture of the man that had escaped from Starlight station.

"Hmm… I'm not sure." He said looking at her.

"Add a fifty-credit tip to the bill."

"Ah, yes, now I remember, Dirk was in a couple of days ago."

"And?"

He looked at her.

"Ok make it a hundred-credit tip."

"Well, I overheard him talking about a big deal and he said he would be back in a day or so."

"Ok, So, he should be back in today. Thanks, we'll hang around for a bit and try and catch him."

She picked up the drinks and headed over to join Datch and Carina sitting at a table at the back. Datch had checked under the seats for bodies but just found bits of glass and a brown sticky patch that might be evolving into a new lifeform. He had made a point of not putting his feet in it in case they dissolved or were eaten.

Kato sat down and handed them the beers.

"Are these safe to drink?" asked Datch looking at the brown liquid in the bottles.

"Yes, they should be. Just don't drink too much of it or it may melt your brain."

Datch took a sip. It didn't taste that bad and was certainly better than the stuff on welly four before the awakening.

Carina watched him take a drink.

'*Is it ok?*' came Carina's voice in his head.

'*Yes, its drinkable.*' He thought back to her.

"I asked the Barman about our friend." Said Kato.

"What did he say?" asked Datch.

"Apparently his name is Dirk and he was in here talking about some great deal he had going."

"Did the barman know if he was coming back?"

"Yes, today he thinks."

"Cool, so we just have to sit and wait then."

"I'll message the others and get them to come here."

Datch fetched out his vid com and messaged Rosey and Krissy.

They took another swallow of the beer.

"Are you sure this stuff won't harm us?" asked Carina screwing up her face.

"Well harm is a general term. I wouldn't drink too much of it or the nanobots in your system are going to be working overtime." said Kato.

"Oh." Carina said and gave the beer a hard stare in an attempt to make it think twice about hurting her.

"So, what are we going to do when he comes in?" asked Datch.

"Hmm. Not sure. We'll have to grab him somehow. I'm sure if myself and Tate can get close enough, we should be able to capture him."

They had another gulp of beer and then concluded that it wasn't beer, but something pretending to be beer.

Datch got out his hand scanner and checked it.

It told him that the beer was drinkable but advised about drinking too much of it.

Just then the door opened and Tate came in with Rosey and Hagger. They looked around and after peering into the darkness for a few seconds spotted them sitting at the back and gave a subtle nod.

They walked over to the bar and got their slightly debus drinks before heading across the room and sitting at the table next to them.

"So, anything?" said Tate glancing at Hagger as if she was talking to him.

"Yes, he's due in here today. The barman thinks we're here the meet him for a business deal." replied Kato.

"Ok. We'll just wait and when he comes in, we'll slowly move towards the door and cut him off." Said Tate.

"OK."

"So, we sit and wait?" asked Hagger.

"Yes."

"What we going to talk about?"

"We could tell Kato and Tate about the skiing a Traxsent."

"Ok."

Datch had just started filling in the background when the door opened and Tish, Krissy, and Dapo came walking in, followed by Timbo. They walked over to the bar, and the barman looked up at Timbo, who was now blocking out the rest of the room.

"Hi, can I help you?"

"Yes, four beers please."

"No problem." said the barman and then noticed the large bag that Timbo was carrying.

"Err... Sorry to ask but what's in the bag?"

Timbo looked at him and grinned.

"My anti-aircraft missile system."

The barman looked at the bag then back at Timbo.

"Err... Try not to use it in here please. I've only just had the last lot of damage repaired."

"No Problem." said Timbo and grinned.

"Where?" asked Krissy.

The barman looked at her and then realised she was actually asking.

"Err, over there and some of the chairs were replaced." He said pointing over the bar.

Krissy looked where he was pointing and realised that part of the wall had been painted, although somewhat badly and a number of stools that appeared to have had their legs splinted with other materials and taped to them with duct tape. Also, there was a very clean area on the carpet that was about the same size as a body.

The barman gave them their beers and they walked over and sat at a table in front of Datch's.

After a sort of covert conversation to bring them up to speed Datch carried on telling the story about Traxsent.

A number of people came in and each time the door opened Kato would casual look over checking to see if it was Dirk.

They sat there for five hours, drinking the so-called beer and telling stories, then just as they were discussing what to do next the door opened and a man walked in. He was around 2 metres high and a medium build. He was wearing a long coat that went down to his knees. Kato was looking at him trying to work out if he was armed.

"I think that's him." she said quietly.

Datch look across the room.

"Yes, he looks like one of the men."

'The guy that's approaching the end of the bar.' He said in Carina's mind.

She looked at Tate and nodded and looked back to the bar.

The man approached the bar and started chatting to the barman. Datch reached forward and tapped Timbo on the shoulder and pointed at the man.

"Ok Datch."

"Be careful, he might be armed."

Timbo got up and started to move towards the door.

The barman pointed across towards Kato and the man turned to look. He spotted Kato and then spotted Tate. He dropped his drink and made a run for the door. Timbo tried to get to him but he was too fast. They all got up and started to run after him.

Datch pressed his ships coms as they ran to the door.

"Clax, he's running. Power up the systems and watch for any ship leaving in a hurry."

"OK Datch, I'm on it."

They reached the door and exited into the street. They looked around and then Rosey shouted.

"Over there!" she said pointing.

Dirk turned and pulled out a gun. Krissy was at the front. Datch spotted the weapon and jumped on Krissy knocking her to the floor as the weapon fired hitting the wall above her.

Krissy looked up into Datch's eyes as was sitting on top of her. She had landed with her legs spread eagled and him sitting in the middle. He looked down.

"Sorry, he was about to shoot you."

"It's ok, Thanks."

He climbed off her and gave her a hand up.

Dirk was running up the street towards the landing area. Datch pulled out his pistol and they started to give chase up the street but there were a lot of people about and the crowd slowed them down. By the time they reached the junction which turned towards the landing area Dirk had vanished.

They stood looking down towards the landing bays checking the scene for any sign of him.

"Let's head back to the ship. He knows we're after him and I bet he won't hang around." said Kato.

"Yes, let's move it." added Datch.

They made their way back to the Raven as fast as they could and had just reached the landing bays when Datch's ships coms beeped.

"Hi Clax, we're nearly back. What's up?"

"A ship has just launched in a hurry."

"He's running guys. Let's move it! Clax, bring everything online, we'll be there in about a minute."

"Ok."

They ran into the landing bay with the Raven in it and straight into the back of the ship. Dapo was last in and pressed the door close switch on the way past. Thirty seconds later Datch slid into the pilot's seat. grabbing his headset in the process.

"Hold on folks!"

He increased thrust and the Raven left the bay heading for the tube leading up the side of the crater and out into space. Behind him everyone scrambled to get in their seats.

Datch continued to increase power as the Raven climbed into darkness of space.

"Do you have him on tactical?" asked Datch as the Raven accelerated up the tube going through forcefield after forcefield. Each flashed brightly as the Raven sped through it. Outside the tube was a blur as they went past.

"Yes, I'll put him in your heads up."

A red dot appeared in front of Datch's eyes.

They reached the end of the tube and were in open space. Datch swung the Raven around as he centred his cross hairs on the dot.

The dot now had numbers at the side of it.

"Looks like he's heading to the asteroids." said Clax.

"Why doesn't he jump to interspace?" asked Carina who was sitting on the edge of her seat.

"I suspect he's scanned us and knows we could keep up and even overtake him. He's going to try and lose in the asteroid belt and then jump to interspace." said Kato.

"Yes, but we can track him, can't we?"

"Yes, but he doesn't know that. Most ships don't have tactical readouts."

The other ship started to move fast and jump sections of space.

"Raven, I need the interspace drive on manual."

"Interspace drive is now on manual."

"Hold on folks."

The stars outside started bending in some very odd ways as Datch went past interspace one. The normal flickering was not happening as the ship was still at low speed and the space was being warped in different directions. Datch was turning this way and that, keeping up with the other ship and the space outside was being stretched and squashed. Also, the ships stabilizers were having a hard time trying to keep the artificial gravity in the downward direction which was making The Pack feel every little movement of the ship. Hagger was starting to look a very funny colour and had gone very quiet.

The asteroid belt was up ahead. The other ship stared to slow down as it entered the asteroids. Datch did the same and the stabilizers started working again. Hagger was glad that down was now normal down and not somewhere else as the dodgy beer he had been drinking had started trying to find its own way out.

The other ship started flying in and out of the asteroids. The Raven was slightly bigger than the other craft and on a couple of occasions Datch had to detour because the gap was too small.

"Clax, can you get a shot on his engines?" said Kato.

"I can't get a lock. He's moving in and out the asteroids too much and the systems don't have time to get a lock on before another rock gets in the way."

"Fire a wide spread of shots and keep repeating it. We won't hit him but it may make him run." said Datch.

Clax bought the forward cannons online and started firing into the asteroids. The other ship started to fly faster catching an asteroid with one of his wings. There was a bright flash as his shields took the brunt of the impact.

"Wow, we were nearly fishing him out of space then."

Another large bolder got in the way and Datch had to dodge it allowing Dirk to pull away a bit. The front shields were flashing as small pebbles got in the way and were vaporised on impact.

"That give me an idea. The next large boulder he dodges behind hit it with all the weapons at once." Said Datch.

"Why?"

"Just do it."

"Ok."

The ships chased through rock after rock and then the other ship ducked down under a large asteroid.

"Now Clax."

All the weapons fired at once. Datch hit full reverse thrust.

"Raven, engage the scattering field!"

The Raven stopped in a shower of exploding rocks.

"What are you doing? He'll get away!" asked Tate.

"Datch is letting him think we hit a rock." Said Kato.

"But he'll come back."

"No, he won't. He won't want to risk us still being able to shoot him."

"Looks like he's slowing." Said Clax.

"Yes. I think he's falling for it."

Datch slowly moved the Raven out of the asteroids and into clear space.

"Err, he's going to see us?" said Tate.

"No, he won't, I turned the scattering field on. He'll only see us if he's gets into visual range. We'll just shadow him at a distance and see where he goes."

"That's good thinking Datch." said Kato.

"I'll take that as a very big compliment."

"What's he doing?"

"It looks like he's scanning the asteroids looking for us."

Datch moved the Raven further away from the asteroids and was now keeping a couple of million kilometres away from him.

"Yes, he's looking for wreckage."

"Err, there isn't any." said Hagger who had got to grips with his stomach at last.

"I know but I'm hoping he won't go to take a look." said Datch who was watching his heads-up display intently.

The other ship hung there for two or three minutes scanning the asteroids for wreckage trying to find the other ship. Dirk was making sure he had enough distance to run if the black ship came after him. Finally, he came to the conclusion that it must be damaged and turned before slowly starting to move away.

"He's moving." said Datch and increased thrust.

He watched the ship making sure he was keeping his distance and matching speed. The ship moved into clear space and stopped.

"What's he doing?" said Carina.

"I'm not sure. He's just sitting there."

"Hmm. maybe he's waiting to see if we come out the belt."

On the other ship, Dirk was looking at his instruments. Yes, there had been an explosion, and then the ship had vanished. But the explosion should have been bigger. He scanned the asteroids again. No sign of a core breach, and no wreckage. He had moved away, and still no pursuit. He gave it one last scan.

'Well, if is still there it's not coming after him. Maybe its impacted on an asteroid and can't move.' He thought to himself.

He decided to head out of the system. He pressed a few buttons and started to power up the interspace drive. He was going to have to keep the speed down, as one of the drive units had suffered damage in the impact. But there was no way he was going back to the base for repairs. That was part of the royal guard who were chasing him, and where there's one, there would be more.

Had something gone wrong with the plan? he wondered. He needed to make a call, but after he was on the move and relatively safe.

Datch watched as the ship turned and then vanished.

"Raven, go to interspace and match speed and heading of the ship targeted in tactical."

The stars outside blinked out and then started to flicker.

Datch sat back in his seat.

"Raven, what is our heading?"

"We are currently on course for Garhar star system."

"Information please on the Garhar star system."

"The Garhar star system is the remains of a system whose star went supernova. It has two planets that survived the explosion on the outer edge of the system. They were both gas giants but now only their rocky cores remain after their thick atmosphere's were blown into deep space by the explosion. The star itself is now a pulsar and shields are required one point five light years out."

"What is the journey time?"

"Time to arrival at current speed, eight hours 6 minutes."

"Thanks Raven, inform me of any change in the target's flight path."

Datch got up and stretched.

"Well, I need some food and a short nap." He said.

"A nap?" said Tate.

"Yes. The ships got this and will tell us of any change. The scattering field will hide us from his sensors so there will be no need for him to change course."

Kato thought about it for a moment.

"I think a break from the cockpit would do us all good. We might need it." she said.

They got up and headed to the rec room for a bite to eat.

Datch and Clax went off and had a nap for a few hours while Kato watched the tactical plot in the cockpit. She was going to wake them if there was any change to the ships heading.

# The Escape

Datch opened his eye and Carina was standing over him calling his name.

"Hi Babes, what's up?" he said looking up.

"We're getting close to the pulsar and it's having a strange effect, Kato said to come and fetch you."

"Ok, I'll be there in a minute."

Carina went off to tell Kato while Datch pulled himself together.

Two minutes later he wandered into the cockpit. Kato looked around as he walked in.

"What's up?"

"Look outside."

He went and sat in his seat and put his headset on. Out of the window he could see small flashes of light.

"That's weird. Raven, please identify the flashes of light outside."

"The flashes of light are being caused by high energy particles hitting the shield. The intensity of the high energy particles will increase as we approach the pulsar."

"Raven, can the other ship see us?"

"No."

"Will the effect make us visible as we approach the star system?"

"Yes, the energy given off will increase to detectable levels by other ships at zero point two five light years from the pulsar."

"Raven, display tactical plot of the Garhar system."

The pulsar appeared in the middle of the cockpit, and then the two planets appeared orbiting at the very edge of the system. The rest of the star system was full of asteroids and debris left over from the star's explosion.

One of the planets started showing high-energy emissions on its surface. Then a ring of satellites appeared around it, along with two small ships. All of them were lit up brightly by the energy bouncing off their shields. There was also another ship on course for the planet. They watched as it reached the planet and then headed into a tunnel on the surface, vanishing from sight.

"There's a base in there." said Datch.

"It's not listed anywhere." said Kato.

"Why would you build a base here? The pulsars energy will make it visible to any ships in the local area."

"That's why. They can see anyone coming almost a light year away. The pulsar lights up any ships shields like a beacon."

"Oh crap. Clax! Get up here. Raven, how long before we are detected."

"The Raven will be visible to the planetary detection array in nineteen minutes."

"Raven drop to interspace five. And update on time detection."

"Now at interspace five. Raven will be detected in seventy-two minutes. Please note: The ship we are currently following is on course for the planet with the high energy signature."

At that point Clax came running into the Cockpit and leaped into his seat.

"What's up?"

"The scattering field is going to be useless in seventy minutes as the pulsars going to light us up like a beacon. There is also some sort of base on one of the planets, and I think it's likely to be full of pirates."

"Oh, that is a problem. So, what's the plan?"

"The plan is we need to come up with one."

"Oh."

"Raven, will we be able to track the ship leaving the star system from here?"

"The pulsars energy emissions will only make it possible to track the ship if exits the system on this side of the pulsar."

"So, if the ship exits the other way, we lose it?"

"Affirmative."

"So, the only way to follow to ship will get us seen because of our shields and he will run for it and I suspect a lot of other ships will come after us. Also, we can't turn the shields off because of the radiation would kill us."

"What are we going to do then?"

Datch sat and looked at the plot. The system was taking a long time to give a detailed image because of the energy from the collapsed star. There wasn't much on it other than a lot of asteroids. The asteroids were being pulled in a decreasing spiral down towards the star. They were most likely the remains of other planets in the system that were destroyed and blown out of the system when the star collapsed. Now, the intense gravity of the pulsar was pulling them back to become part of the star itself.

"I know this will sound mad but what if we used an asteroid as a shield."

"What do you mean?"

"Well, what if we move up behind a small one and push it a long in front of us with the front shields? The shields would be behind it so they would not light up."

"It may work but it's going to take a lot to keep it in front of us. They also move very slowly."

"What if we extend the interspace field around the asteroid?"

"Well, it's possible."

"Ok, Raven please identify asteroids that are about the same size as the Raven."

A number of green circles appeared around the floating points of light in the plot. Datch looked hard at them for a while and then poked one. It expanded out showing a small piece of rock.

"What about that one? It's already moving quite fast and looks like it will take us close to the second planet."

"Ok, say we get there, then what?"

"We can sit on the planets dark side and wait. We can keep both the scattering field and the shields up there without being seen."

"It might work." said Clax.

"You do realise that we will be seen as soon as we move from behind the planet and we don't know how many ships are in the base." said Kato.

"Yes, but when we move, we'll be heading out of the system."

"OK. Let's give it a go."

"Raven, change course to rendezvous with the asteroid highlighted in the tactical plot."

Datch pressed the ships comms.

"Guys, you need to get up here."

The next twenty minutes were spent explaining to the rest of the Pack what they were about to do and starting to get the systems ready. They arrived at the asteroid and Datch manoeuvred the Raven so close to the asteroid you could almost reach out and touch it.

"Raven, increase power to the front shields and extend the interspace field around the asteroid in front of the ship."

"Shield power has been increased to one hundred and twenty percent. I am unable to comply with the interspace field. Such adjustments are not recommended and must be carried out manually."

"Raven, give me interspace control at my command." said Clax.

The vid in front of Clax lit up showing the interspace field, generators and field strengths.

"I've got this Datch, you do the shields."

"Ok. here we go."

Datch moved the Raven so that flashes of light could be seen coming off the surface of the rock. Then he started to increase thrust. Warning lights started to flash.

"I need more power, taking the replicators and other non-essential systems offline."

"Sorry, no more Solar Ball folks." said Dapo sarcastically.

"I thought that was an essential system." Said Tish.

Datch transferred more power to the front shields balancing them so that no one emitter was taking more load than the others. The warning lights changed to amber and then the Raven started to move the rock forward slowly increasing speed. It took a while to get up to interspace transit speed and even then, they were only going to get interspace four at best.

"Ok Clax, Ready when you are."

"Ok, here we go."

The stars outside the ship started to bend and twist is some very strange ways.

"I need some more power."

"Ok."

Datch pressed some virtual buttons and rerouted some of the power from the rear shields.

"How's that?"

"Better, the fields starting to stabiles."

The stars outside stared to become streaks of light instead of flickering and then became a series of dots that jumped backwards and forwards.

"There, we're at interspace four. But I'm having to keep adjusting the field. Try to keep the speed constant if you can."

"Ok. I'll try my best but the density of the rock is making the thrusters overheat a bit and I keep having to back them off."

"How long till we reach the planet?"

"About 2 hours. Kato, can you watch the tactical plot for us. This is taking a lot of work to keep it stable."

"Warning interspace field is working outside of operating parameters. Instability could occur."

"Raven, please disable alarms for interspace drive while it is under manual control." said Datch.

"Alarms for interspace drive disabled. Warning forward shield emitters are overheating."

"And the ones for the front shield!"

"Alarms for front shields disabled."

They battled with the ship for about fifty minutes before things started to calm down.

"I think we're stable now. The shield emitters are stable and running at one hundred and five percent. How's it over there?"

"The interspace field is stable ish. I'm not having to do much in the way of adjustment now."

The atmosphere in the cabin started to relax a bit.

"Can we get up?" asked Rosey.

"Yes, but don't use any of the ships systems. All the power is being used to keep us stable. And I mean none. Don't even flush the toilet."

"I think I'll stay here." said Carina.

"Kato, what's the other ship doing?"

"It's just about to enter the base."

"I bet he will be there for a while. He'll need to refuel and maybe even repair the damage from the asteroid belt."

"How's our fuel looking?"

"The fuel level is about halfway. Hopefully we can catch him before we need to refuel."

The next hour and a half were intense as Clax and Datch flew the ship on a knife-edge. Every now and then, lights would flash and adjustments would be made. The journey to the safety of the planet seemed like an eternity, and every minute that passed by was dragged out across space. Finally, they made it to the planet.

"OK Clax, time to lose this extra weight."

"Disengaging interspace in 5. 4. 3. 2. 1."

The stars turned back to normal and Datch reversed thrust. The asteroid started to move slowly way from the front on the ship.

"Raven put all systems back to automatic and engage the scattering field."

"All systems are now back to normal operation. Scatting field is now engaged."

Datch brought the Raven into a stationary position behind the planet and then relaxed.

"Ok, We're good. Raven display tactical on the cockpit holo emitters."

The star system appeared in the cockpit and they sat looking at it. Nothing was happening, apart from a couple of fighters doing a few laps around the planet. It was looking like the base hadn't detected them. They watch it for a while before deciding to take it in turns to watch the plot. Tate took the first watch while the others all went for a break and to use the bathroom at last.

The next eight hours went by without anything at all. Datch and Clax had another nap and the rest of The Pack did the same.

Then six small ships came into the system in a cone shaped formation. They flew around the planet a couple of times before going into the base. Just after they arrive another larger ship appeared and headed straight to the base.

Datch walked into the cockpit and Kato was sitting watching it.

"Anything?" he said going over to her.

"I think a raiding party came in a bit ago with a cargo ship, but the pirate ships were in a fighter wing pattern, which was a bit odd. They're normally a bit more random than that. Otherwise, it's been very quiet."

"No sign of our friend?"

"No, he's still in the base."

"Are you still ok for a bit?"

"Yes. I'm good."

"Ok, I'll grab a bite to eat. Do you want anything?"

"I'll have a sandwich if possible?"

"Jeader ok?"

“Sure.”

Datch headed back to the rec room for food.


Inside the planet, below a thousand feet of rock, was a base. It had landing bays, a repair and maintenance area, and a living complex. It was about the size of a small town and had a sense of military precision about it. In the centre of it was a brightly lit bar.

Dirk sat in the bar talking with a group of men.

“A black ship that was like a ghost?” said one of the men.

“Yes, It’s after me.”

“Are you sure it’s here and you’re not being paranoid?”

“No, I’m not sure but I have a feeling it’s watching me.”

“Well, the perimeter scans show nothing other than a few small asteroids. Are you sure it was them?”

“Yes, it was the two bodyguards and the males who caught us getting the Jackar.”

“Hmm. well, I think you’re just imaging things but we’ll give you an escort out of the system if it will make you happy.”

The man turned to a couple of other men sitting on the next table.

“You two, wait ten minutes after Dirk launches and then follow him for a couple of light years before coming back. If you see anything following him destroy it.”

“Yes, sir.”

“Dirk, you make sure you deliver the Jackar to our courier or our ladyship with not be happy. You have all the to courier details and the fake ID’s?”

"Yes, I have all the stuff including the fake implant emitters. I won't fail you."

"You had better not or we're all going to wish we were dead. Are you ready to depart?"

"If it's ok, I'll have on more drink and then make a move."

"Is your ship, ok?"

"Yes, the repair teams have repaired the wing and the interspace drive for me. They have done a great job, thanks.

"Is you fuel, ok?"

"Yes thanks. The crew refuelled it as well when they did the repairs."

"Good."

They sat and talked a bit more while Dirk finished off his drink and then it was time to depart.


On the Raven the comms beep and Kato told everyone hurry up and come to the cockpit.

Datch and Clax came running into the cockpit and jumped into their seats.

"Where is he?" said Datch putting his headset on.

"He has just launched from the base and is getting ready to jump to interspace."

"Ok give him a minute to go to interspace and then we'll follow. Raven as soon as the target ship jumps to interspace locate its destination."

They watched until the ship went to interspace.

"Targets course is on a heading to Klayton star system."

"That's the star system next to Thoth where we're doing the gig." said Clax.

"Ok Clax, bring the weapons online. As soon as we move the base will see us."

"Weapons are hot."

"Hold on folks!"

Datch pulled back on the thrust control and the Raven appeared from behind the planet. The shields lit up like an exploding firework as the high energy particles from the pulsar hit it. At the same time two ships launched from the space station.

"Looks like we have company!" said Kato as the two ships headed straight for the Raven.

Datch turn the Raven and went to interspace following Dirk's ship.

The two ships followed them and were gaining on the Raven.

"Can we go any faster?"

"Yes, but we'll lose Dirk's ship if we do and if he changes course that will be it. How long before the other ships reach us?"

The Raven shuddered as the rear shield was hit by a bolt of energy.

"Err, about now!"

"Ok let's give as good as we get. Open Fire!"

Clax started firing at the lead ship lighting its forward shields up.

Another bolt of energy hit the Raven's shields, then another and another as the second ship got into range.

The Raven was being rocked as hit after hit landed on the shields.

"Clax!"

Alarms started flashing in the cockpit. The lead ship's front shield finally gave way under the onslaught from the Raven's pulse canons and there was an explosion as the next bolt hit the front of the ship destroying its forward canon and damaging part of the hull. Clax hit it again and fire erupted from one of its engines and it started to spin out of control dropping out of interspace as it did.

Another bolt of energy rocked the Raven. Datch was battling with the controls as the Raven rocked from side to side. It was bad enough trying to dodge canon fire in normal space when the ship was easy to handle but in interspace the ship handled like an elephant on roller-skates.

Clax was now firing all four pulse canons at the second ship then there was a loud bang and the tactical plot vanished.

"Oh Shit! The weapons are offline along with tactical."

Timbo got up and went running out of the cockpit.

"I think their front shield is down. I'm trying to reroute power to get the weapons back online."

Another bolt hit the rear shield and more alarms started sounding.

"OH crap! I'm losing interspace."

Down in the cargo bay Timbo put on a space suit and opened his bag. He started depressurising the bay.

"Dam! The cargo bay is depressurising." Shouted Datch.

"Are we going to die?" shouted Rosey.

"Not if I can help it!" shouted Datch.

Down in the cargo bay Timbo opened the rear door and lifted up the anti-aircraft missile system. The target display locked on to the other ship and he pressed the fire button. Raven shuddered as an anti-aircraft missile shot out of the back of the ship pushing Timbo backwards across the cargo bay in the process. The missile streaked across space and hit the other ship in the interspace engine.

There was a huge explosion as the other ship exploded into a thousand pieces when the lines of energy inside its interspace engine collapsed in on themselves. Timbo smiled and closed the door.

"What just happened?" asked Datch.

"Err, it looks like the other ship just exploded."

"Did you hit it?"

"No, I don't have the weapons back online yet."

Datch sat pressing buttons, rerouting this system and that one. Then Timbo came walking back in with a grin on his face.

They all looked at him.

"I have taken care of things." He said smiling.

"You did that?" asked Kato.

"Yes, I used my anti-aircraft missile system. I knew it would be useful."

"Timbo. You're amazing." said Rosey.

"Thanks Timbo. You're a star." Shouted Datch while frantically pressing buttons.

Datch finally shut the last alarm up and relaxed a bit.

"How are we looking?" asked Kato.

"Well, the tactical system is dead and one of the interspace drives is not working correctly. Weapons are back up but we lost one of the pulse canons. Other than that, we're looking ok."

"Where's Dirk?" asked Tate.

"He's gone and without tactical, we can't track him."

"So, what now?"

"We head to Klayton and hope he's there when we arrive. We can only do interspace fourteen at best and that's if the damaged engine holds together so I'm going to keep the speed a bit lower. Raven set course for Klayton interspace twelve."

"Do you wish standard alarm?"

"Yes please. Engage."

The stars outside stared to flicker.

"Clax, can you go to the engine room and try to sort out some of the damage. I'll stop here and keep an eye on the systems and try to fix as much as I can from this end."

"Sure thing."

"I'll come with you." said Fred.

"Ok folks, go and chill. We're good for now."

The Pack got up and headed out of the cockpit.

Kato sat looking at Datch.

"What?" he said.

"You are quite a team, aren't you?"

"We are family." he said.

"Yes, you are." she said and smiled before getting up and following the rest to the rec room.

Twenty minutes later Datch was just starting to relax when another warning light started to flash.

He activated the ships coms.

"Clax, what's up? I'm getting an overload warning."

"Yes, it looks like a system behind the wall panel in Krissy room. You'll have to get it. I'm fighting a power drain in the reactor shielding at the moment."

"Ok, I'm on it!"

Datch jumped out his seat and went running down to Krissy's room.

He went charging into her room and crossed over to the panel. He opened it and pulled the power coupling out. The system warning light on the panel started showing green. Datch relaxed and turned around just as Krissy came walking out of the shower. She was totally naked and Datch's jaw dropped at the sight of her body.

She stopped and looked at him.

"There was an overload and I had to stop it. Err, sorry I didn't know you were, err naked." he said looking at the power coupling that he was holding.

She picked up a towel from the bed and wrapped it around her.

"Don't be, from what Carina has told me you have seen me naked before."

"She has?"

"Yes, on Earth when you were getting me dressed. She said you had a good look."

Datch started to blush.

"Yes, your, err, body, was very interesting."

Datch was feeling a little unconfutable.

"That's not quite what she said but I don't mind really. Here look."

She opened the towel flashing her body at him. Datch swallowed hard and went even more red. She laughed and closed the towel.

"Just to let you know I've seen you naked to."

"You have?"

"Yes. You shouldn't use the main bathroom at home unless you're going to put something on first."

"Oh."

"And just to let you know, you have a pretty interesting body too."

Datch went very red and Krissy smiled and then changed the subject.

"By the way, did you know my shower has stopped working?"

Datch looked down at the power coupling again and then back at Krissy.

"Yes, I think you might have to use the one in the spare room."

"OK, but I think I'll be fine for a while."

He stood looking at her for a moment unsure what to do.

"Err, do you want to watch me get dressed by any chance?"

"Err, oh, err, no. I need to go back to the cockpit."

"I bet you do." she said and laughed again.

"OK, see you later." he said.

He left the room in a hurry and headed back to the cockpit. He was feeling very hot and flustered all of a sudden.

He loved Carina with all of his heart but there was something primeval about Krissy that made him want her.

He sat down in the pilot's seat and pressed the coms button.

"Clax, I fixed the overload in Krissy's room. It was the power coupling but her shower doesn't work anymore."

"How do you know her shower doesn't work?"

"She was in it at the time."

"Oh, is she ok?"

"Yes, she just, err, needed her towel."

"O.K. Are there any more warnings?"

"No. Everything is looking good or amber."

"Good, I've sorted the power drain out I think so we're ok for now."

"I'll stay here for a bit and keep an eye on things. You go and chill for a bit."

"OK Datch."

With that the coms closed.

Datch sat with his thoughts going over what had just happened. Was Krissy flirting with him. It felt like she was. She was very attractive and seemed to be encouraging him. It was like a forbidden fruit. Carina would kill him if he went with her. He decided to put her out of his mind and just focus on the task at hand which was getting them to Klayton.

# Klayton

It took three days to get to Klayton at interspace twelve. During which Clax and Fred managed to stabilise the interspace drive and bypassed all the damaged systems.

The Pack were all in the rec room when the alarm went off. Datch and Clax got up and headed to the cockpit.

Datch put on his headset and turned to Clax.

"I think we'll go to the space port in the capital. It will have everything needed to fix the Raven and also, I suspect that if Dirk is still there, he'll be in the city."

"Yes, but please make sure we're at 100% before giving chase again."

"I will, that was a bit on the rough side."

"You can say that again."

Datch turned to the front.

"Klayton control. This is the Raven on approach to Tillar requesting beacon."

"Good morning, Raven. Please transmit you ID's and cargo manifest."

Datch pressed a few virtual buttons.

"IDs transmitted. We have no cargo. Can you inform the space port we will need some repairs as we ran into a couple of pirate ships on route and took a bit of damage."

"Raven, can you land safely?"

"Yes, most systems are working ok."

"I will inform them and have them bring you into the service yard. Has anyone sustained any injuries?"

"No control, just a few jangled nerves."

"OK Raven. Lock on to beacon 220908."

Datch pressed a few more buttons.

"Control, we're locked on to beacon."

"Copy that, Raven. Control out."

The rest of The Pack slowly appeared and sat down.

The Raven dropped out of interspace and there in front of them was a red and brown world with an orange tint in the atmosphere. In orbit around it sat two space stations orbiting on opposite sides of the planet. Down below an ocean covered the lower part of the surface and cities could be seen spread out across the continent. The vegetation was a brown, purple colour because the star gave off more light in the infrared spectrum and therefore the plants had evolved to make use of the stars light.

Datch dropped the Raven down through the atmosphere into an orange sky with cream-coloured clouds. Below was a large forest that gave way into fields laid out like a like a patchwork quilt on the surface of the world. Then in the distance a city could be seen, it was sprawled out across the county side like a large concrete jungle with the spaceport sitting at its centre.

"Tillar Control. This is Raven on approach to the spaceport. Requesting landing instructions."

"Raven. This is Tillar control, head to pad 42. We understand you require repairs?"

"Affirmative Control. We had a bit of a run it with some pirates."

"Raven, a member of the maintenance team will be waiting for you when you land."

"Thanks Control. Five minutes to pad."

The Raven approached the city flying over the buildings and descending as it went. The spaceport was a large area with around two hundred landing pads at least. The maintenance area was to right side of the main landing area and was half empty having only a few ships in it and it looked like they were only being refuelled.

Datch spotted pad 42 and brought the Raven in for a gentle landing and then shut the systems down.

"Well folks, I think we're going to be here a while so let's go and find a hotel."

"Yes, and after that I think a bar is needed." Added Clax.

They got up and head down to the cargo bay. Collecting their overnight bags on route. They entered the cargo bay and laying on the floor next to one of the bikes was Timbo's Anti-aircraft missile system.

"Err, Timbo. It may be an idea to put that back in your bag. They may try to mount it somewhere otherwise."

"Good point Datch. I might need it again."

He went over to it and picked it up before stuffing it in the very large bag that he had used to carry it around.

"Right. let's head out."

Datch opened the door and they walked down the ramp. He looked up at the underside of the Raven and on the left side near the left interspace engine was a large hole with cables hanging out. Datch looked around. There was another hole near the front on the under belly of the hull.

"Ouch." Said Fred looking at the holes.

"You can say that again." Said Tank.

"That is going to take a while to fix." Added Clax.

The attendant came over to them.

"Good morning, sir. Control informed us that you needed some repairs. I can see you need quite a few."

"Yes, we ran into a couple of pirates on the way here and we took quite a beating. The left interspace drive has taken a hit and the ship's tactical system is offline. Also, one of the pulse cannons is not working."

"You were lucky to escape. Would you like me to call the security services to report them?"

"No. Let's just say the pirates are walking home without spacesuits."

"Oh, I see, sir. I'm sure they deserved the exercise."

He fetched out a scanner and scanned the damaged sections. The unit beeped and listed the issues.

"Looking at this, it's going to take a couple of days to fix it all. It will be about thirty thousand credits, give or take a thousand."

"No problem. If you touch up the paint as well, I'll add a thousand credit tip for you and your crew."

The attendant smiled.

"Thank you, sir. I will expedite repairs for you. If you could just give me your vid com ID data so I may contact you when the repairs are complete."

Datch looked at the attendant's vid com and it beeped. "Thank you, sir. Is there anything else?"

"Yes. Can you recommend a good hotel by any chance? The price is not important."

"The Grand Hall is really nice but it is expensive. I think it's the third stop on the transit tube into the city sir."

"Thank you. How do we get out?"

"You can exit through the main spaceport over there. I'll message you when the repairs are complete."

"Thank you again."

They turned and headed towards the main building. Behind them they heard the attendant yell, 'Hey Jait, drop that, this one's an important job. The beers are on me when it's done!'

They walked through the spaceport and up to the high-speed transit system. This world was quite different to most of the ones they normally went to. There were no green plants, everything was an orange or brown with a few deep reds thrown in for good measure. The buildings were creams, reds, or browns. Not the bright colours they were used to. Everything was coloured to make the most of the light from the star. Datch wondered what they were going to make of the gig in two weeks' time when they started glowing bright green.

They exited the transit system and walked down the steps into the street below. The light level was similar to an evening on Bellatrix, but it was lunchtime. This was due to the star emitting more light in the infrared spectrum and at levels and wavelengths different to the Bellatrixian star.

The Grand Hall was two hundred metres down the street from the transit stop. It had a brightly coloured front which set it apart from the rest of the buildings around it. They walked inside and up to the reception desk.

The receptionists look over the deck at them.

"Good afternoon, ladies and gentlemen. How may I help you?"

"We would like twelve rooms please. Three doubles and the rest singles."

"How long are you staying?"

"We think two nights but maybe three."

"It will cost one thousand four hundred credits per night. Is that all right, sir?"

"That's great. Thank you."

They all stepped forward one at a time to be booked in.

An hour later, they were all standing in the hotel bar, having a beer.

"So, what now?" asked Tate.

"I'm not sure," said Kato. "But I suspect Dirk is coming here to meet with someone, or he would have stayed at the pirate's base where it was safe until the heat was off."

"Maybe we should go and check out some of the local bars and see if there's one where a Dirk is hanging out? I want to talk to him about a number of holes in my paintwork," said Datch in a very sarcastic tone.

"Yes, and I want to talk to him about my underwear," added Hagger.

They all turned to look at him.

"Well, I need new ones."

"You really shouldn't say things like that in public," said Rosey.

"Why?"

"It's not cool, dude," said Peebop.

"Oh. Well, I do need to buy some more." With that, he went quiet.

"So, moving on, let's head into the city. Timbo, we won't be needing the anti-aircraft missile system, so you won't need to fetch it."

"Okay, Datch," he said, looking a little disappointed.

Datch started to wonder if he was likely to start carrying it around with him. He hoped not.

"Everyone, drink up. We need to find a seedy bar."

They finished their drinks and headed out into the city.

The afternoon was bright by Klayton standards but more like a dull day on Bellatrix. They walked to the transport tubes and entered one of the carriages heading to the downtown area. This according to the city guides was the area where the bulk of the bars were.

The downtown area was lit up with bright lights shining across the streets from all the shops, restaurants and bars. All of them trying to entice you inside.

They came to the first bar and went in. The inside was brightly coloured and very well-lit. It had a dance floor at the back with a DJ booth to one side. It looked like it was a happening sort of place, with music playing quite loudly. They bought a round of drinks and went and sat near the door so they could hear each other talk. This was more important for Datch and Carina now, as the whole telepathy thing had worn off because they hadn't had a gig for over two weeks. This was a bonus for the rest of the Pack, as now they could hear the whole conversation and not just bits and pieces.

"Well, this is not very seedy." said Dapo.

"More up market I think." said Tish.

"Yes, the sort of place we could hang out." Added Rosey.

"I like it." said Krissy.

"I can't see Dirk coming in here." said Hagger.

Kato looked at them for a moment.

"Why do you think he wouldn't come in here?"

"It's not seedy." said Rosey.

"What if he thinks we are still looking for him. He wouldn't go to a seedy bar in case we were there."

They stopped and thought for a moment.

"So, you're saying that he won't be in a seedy bar because he thinks we will."

"Err, no."

"So, he will?"

"No. I'm saying he could be in any of the bars and we don't even know he is here."

"Kato's right." said Tank. "He might not be here. We had better go slow with the beers and work our way around all the bars. With tactical down he could have passed us going the other way and we wouldn't have even seen him."

Datch was looking into space for a moment before snapping back into reality.

"Well, there are thirty-nine bars in the city. So, we've got a few to go through." he said.

"I'm up for that!" said Krissy smiling at Datch.

"Well, that's going to take two or three days to get round them all and that's if we only have one drink in each of them." said Clax.

"Well, I'm thinking sixteen pints in one day is a good work out for my liver." Said Krissy and winked at Datch.

Datch had no idea what her liver had to do with it and put it down to being an Earth thing that involved lots of beer drinking. He winked back at her and she smiled.

"So, what do we do?" asked Fred.

"We could split up again?" said Hagger.

"I'm not sure that is a wise idea. If we were on our own and if he recognises us, he won't think twice about killing us. The pirates have already tried it once and he shot at Krissy in the Tray system."

"That's a good point."

They sat thinking and looking at their drinks.

"Well, let's have a tour of the bars anyway."

"I think we should head to the next two and then find one with food." said Carina.

"Sounds like we have a plan." Said Krissy.

They sat and finished their drinks before moving on to the next bar. The next bar was a lot seedier, with subtle lighting and the barman had a lot of tattoos, which made it seedy according to Hagger. They bought a round of drinks and sat looking around the bar. Krissy also seemed to be paying Datch a bit more attention than normal. He wasn't sure, but he started to think she was flirting with him again.

They moved from bar to bar. Some of them were big, posh bars full of aliens from other worlds, and were brightly lit. Others were small, dimly lit affairs that catered for the local population of the planet. The normal light levels were much lower than on other worlds, and this meant that the indigenous population liked darker areas, as that was what their eyes had adapted to.

At each bar they went into, they would have a good look around, and then Kato would show the bar staff an image of Dirk and ask if they had seen him. There was a lot of head shaking. The first few bars didn't take very long, but as the afternoon turned to evening, it started to take longer in each bar. By mid-evening, it was taking over an hour, as the alcohol was taking effect.

By the end of the day, they had been through seventeen bars, a large amount of beer, lots of hack's wings, a number of pizzas, not to mention all the crisps and nuts that they had eaten. They decided just after midnight that it was time to head back to the hotel, and ordered a taxi to take them, as they couldn't remember where the hotel was, or for that matter, how to get to wherever it was.

When Datch and Carina got back to their room, Carina turned on Datch.

"Datch, what's going on between you and Krissy?"

He looked at her unsure about what to say.

"Err, I'm not sure?"

"Not sure? she's been flirting with you all day."

"Yes, I had noticed. But I don't know how to handle it. She is living with us and I don't want to cause friction with her."

Carina gave Datch a long hard look and was wishing that the telepathy thing was working.

"I know you fancy her. You have done since we found her." she said.

"Err, I sort of do, but I love you."

"Well, Rosey has noticed and was watching you. As was I."

"What am I meant to do?"

Datch was starting to feel the heat. This was the first time he had ever had a proper grilling from Carina and it didn't feel good.

"Hmm…" said Carina walking over to the window. She stopped and stood looking out into the city while pondering the thoughts in her head.

Datch waited for a minute and then cautiously said "Carina?"

She turned and looked at him. She didn't look angry which seemed to make things feel worst.

Carina came to a decision.

"Well, I quite like her too." She said and paused.

Datch stood looking at her not knowing what to say or do.

"OK, I love you very much too. But let's add a bit of spice to our relationship."

Datch was really wishing he could read her thoughts right now.

"What are you thinking?" he said trying to work out what was going on.

"Ask her if she wants a relationship with both of us. I'm sure it would be interesting if nothing else."

"What? You fancy her too?"

"Yes, a bit. Let's see if it will work. If it doesn't, we'll have to come up with plan B."

Datch stood trying to take in what Carina had just said. His dad did have a number of wives and a couple of husbands that overlapped each other but he did say it was hard work handling a five-way relationship. Still, this would be just three ways.

"OK." he said, "but, how are we going to ask her?"

"Well, she's flirting with you. You can do it and make sure she knows I'm up for it to. Just try to get the timing right though."

"I'll try." said Datch who was slightly shocked.

"Ok, Now let's get in bed. I might not have you to myself much longer." She grinned and then pulled his shirt over his head before running into the bedroom.


The following day, they had breakfast before starting the pub crawl again at around eleven ish. They headed to the next bar on the list.

At midday, Datch's vid com bleeped. He fetched it out of his pocket and looked at it. It was a message from the spaceport.

"Timbo, the spaceport wants to know if we want them to mount the missile system on the Raven. Is that the one you were carrying or the new one?"

"Err, the one I was carrying. You can have it mounted if you like, Datch."

"Yes, it might be an idea," Clax added.

Datch messaged them back to say, "Yes, please," and then they returned to the matter in hand. Timbo started staring into space again.

They spent all day zigzagging across the city, finding all the seedy bars in the process, along with a couple of restaurants for food. But finally, they had managed to cover all the remaining bars by mid-evening.

The last one they ended up in was called The Caverns. It had been created in a large cavern that was part of the natural caves under the city. The acoustics were amazing. They sat watching as a band played on the stage.

As far as finding Dirk was concerned, it looked like the trail had gone cold.

"So, what now?" asked Tate.

Datch looked at her for a moment.

"The Raven should be fixed tomorrow so maybe we can use tactical to find out if the ship is here. All that time following it has given the system a very refined imprint of its energy signature. We'll be able to find it without its ID beacon if it's in the local area."

"I'll Contact the Princess and see if she knows anything else." Said Kato.

"I'm starting to think we're at a dead end." said Fred.

"Yes, me too." Added Tank.

"We can't just give in." said Datch.

"Datch, we have no leads and the chances of finding the ship are very remote."

Fred could see the look of disappointment on Datch's face.

"Look, we'll give it another couple of days and then if we are still at a dead end then we head to the resort for the rest of the break and chill out."

Datch looked at them. He didn't like to give up but he knew they were right and they couldn't keep going, hoping that they would get a break.

"OK, two more days and then if we don't have a lead we'll stop. Sorry Kato, but we are running out of time and with no leads we have to stop at some point. If you need a lift somewhere we'll take you."

"You have risked so much to help us. We can't thank you enough for all your help even if we don't find him."

"Well, let's just hope we can find a lead before we have to go."

"I'll drink to that." said Peebop.

The band started playing some rock style tunes and most of The Pack got up to dance.

They were now in party mode, and after a couple more beers, Datch sat down next to Krissy while the others were dancing.

"Krissy, I know this might seem a bit of an awkward question, but do you fancy me?"

Krissy looked at him, unsure of what was going on.

"Look, I don't mind if you do. But I need to know." He added.

"Yes, I do a bit, but you have Carina."

Datch smiled.

"Well, this is not Earth, we don't have the same taboos as they do on that planet."

"What do you mean?" she asked. She had been brought up with the mindset that you find a man, have children, and then live together until you die.

"Well, as we have told you, we live for seven thousand of your Earth years, and therefore we have multiple partners. It is pretty much normal to have a couple of wives and husbands all at once."

"Oh, so what are you saying?"

"Carina spotted you looking at me yesterday."

"Oh, did you have and argument about me?"

Datch laughed.

"I thought it was going to be one but no, she quite fancies you too. So, we were wondering if you would be interested in being part of our relationship."

"You're asking me to have a date with you and Carina?"

"Err, I suppose so, yes. The only way it will work is if it's a three-way relationship. We have both decided that if you want to give it a go, we will?"

"Err, can I think about it?"

"Sure."

He leant forward and kissed her.

"That's on account." He smiled and sat back in his chair.

She looked at him still trying to think things through. Yes, she liked him and had wondered what it would be like to be with him. She had never thought about Carina though, but the idea of it did sound interesting. But what if it didn't work. She wasn't sure.

"I'm going up to dance. Do you want to come?"

"Err, ok."

They got up and headed across to the others. They started dancing next to Carina, Rosey and Tish. After a couple of minutes Datch whispered in Carina's ear and told her that he had asked Krissy about the three some.

Carina then started dancing with Krissy. When the next song started Datch headed off to the toilet before going back to his seat. He sat watching the girls having fun and started to wonder what life was going to be like now there might be three of them. Very, very complicated he decided.

He got another round of drinks and then headed back to the dancefloor.

Carina was dancing quite close to Krissy by the end of the night along with Datch.

The night came to an end and they headed back to the hotel. Datch and Carina walked Krissy back to her hotel room and stopped at her door. Carina turned to Krissy and kissed her on the lips. Then Datch not wanting to be left out did the same.

"Have a think about what you want." Said Carina.

"Yes, I'm sure we can work it out if you want to try it." Added Datch.

"I'll think about it." Said Krissy.

She went in the room and closed the door.

Kissy got undressed and got into bed. She lay there thinking about Datch and Carina. It sounded interesting and the idea of the three of them together would make things fun if nothing else. But what if it went wrong, what then. She turned over and took her hangover pill before settling down to sleep.

The next morning, they sat in the hotel bar after breakfast, mulling over what to do. Kato was looking at her vid com with a puzzled expression. Datch noticed and had to ask.

"Kato, is everything alright?" he asked.

She looked at him for a moment before answering.

"Erm, yes. I just got a bit of an odd message from the Princess."

"What does it say?"

"She seemed to think we were dead and was surprised to hear from me."

"Why?"

"I don't know. Maybe someone in the palace told her that we'd been killed. But why someone would do that, I don't know. Information can be a bit disjointed at times in the royal court, so it could have just been a miscommunication."

"Oh. What else did she say?"

"Well, she doesn't have any more information for us on the pirates. The intelligence services have been coming up empty. Also, the king is coming under more and more pressure to abdicate over the Jackar thing. The people are saying that if he can't look after his own daughter then he should step down."

"Sounds like things aren't going well. What happens if he steps down?" asked Fred.

"The Princess will have to step up, as he doesn't have any male heirs. So, her wanting to be able to go out by herself will come to an abrupt end."

"Oh, well. Let's just hope we find a lead before it's too late."

"What's the plan for today?" Rosey asked.

"Hmm, we've been to all the bars, so he's not here. Well, at least not yet, or we've missed him," Clax said.

Datch looked at Kato. "Which one do you think he'd go in if he came here?" he asked.

"Well, I don't think it would be a seedy one," Kato said.

"Why not?" Hagger asked. He quite liked going into the rough bars.

"We found him in one last time. He'll go to an upmarket one, assuming we'll be looking in the seedy ones for him," Tate said.

"Oh, that's clever," Hagger added, looking thoughtful.

"That rules out about a third of the bars in the city. What else?" Clax asked.

"I doubt it will be the high-end bars either, as the prices for drinks are very expensive and there's normally a dress code. By the way, why did they let us in those?" Kato asked, looking at Datch.

"Err, we have a reputation, and the doormen were very pleased with their tips for opening the doors for us," he said.

"You tipped them to let us in?" Tate asked.

"Yes."

"Okay, so rule out the high-end ones. So that leaves about fifteen?"

"Maybe, thereabouts."

"I think they're likely to be nearer to the spaceport than on the other side of the city. He won't want to be too far away from his ship," Peebop said.

Datch pulled out his vid com and pulled up a city map. He placed it on the table in front of them.

"Vid com, please display all the bars in the city."

Little symbols appeared on the map.

"Remove any bars that require a dress code."

A number of the symbols disappeared.

"Remove all the bars that have a high crime rate."

About half the symbols now vanished.

"How far from the spaceport are we thinking?" he asked.

"Hmm, say fifteen minutes travel time. I would want to get back to my ship fast if things went wrong," Clax said.

"Vid com, remove all bars that are more than fifteen minutes travel time from the spaceport using public transport."

Only five bars were left on the screen.

"Okay, looks like we have five left. The Ranger, Tillar Palace, Nemo's, Star city and The Kingdom."

Kato looked at them on the map.

"I think Tillar Palace," she said.

"Why?"

"Well, there is a transit point right outside that goes straight to the spaceport, and it also has a wide-open front that gives a clear view up and down the street. Add to that the fact that it will be a busy bar because of its proximity to the spaceport, and therefore, it is a pretty good place to come where he would not be easily seen."

"Okay. We'll head there for now. It's a nice bar if nothing else," Datch said.

They finished the last sips of their coffee and headed to the bar.

# The Drop

Above Klayton, the two space stations followed their orbits, keeping themselves in geostationary position on opposite sides of the planet. One sat almost directly above the capital city. It was as large as a city and cylindrical in shape, with a docking ring halfway down that wrapped around the outside to enable large ships such as starliners to dock. At its centre was another docking portal that led to docking bays for smaller ships and shuttles from the planet. Inside, the main habitation areas consisted of parks, shops, bars, restaurants, hotels, and also a large commerce area with a cargo storage facility.

Dirk sat in one of the bars, looking down at the planet below. He had been there for a couple of days, waiting for a courier to contact him. The courier would give him the location for the transfer of the Jackar, and more importantly, his credits.

He watched as a starship flew past the window, heading down to the surface. His thoughts shifted back to the haunting image of the black ship. The last the base had heard was that it was taking heavy damage, and then the attacking ships had stopped transmitting. The base had tried to locate the ships, but to no avail, and they were assumed to be lost.

He had taken a long way around coming from the other side of the star to make sure it was not following him. He even sat in orbit for a couple of hours just in case and still nothing. After he was sure it wasn't nearby, he entered the space station and checked into the hotel as planned.

There was still something worrying him, though. He had a feeling it was still out there somewhere, waiting for him. He shuddered at the thought of it coming out of the darkness of space towards him. He looked at his drink before taking a good gulp of the spirit. It was like a wraith appearing from nowhere. There had been nothing on his ship's sensors, and then there it was, following him. It just appeared out of nowhere. He shuddered again and took another gulp from his drink.

Hopefully, the courier would call soon so he could get the hell out of here. He would feel better once he was halfway across the galaxy.

This was meant to be an easy job, and it would set him up with enough credits so he could head to another part of the galaxy and start again. He didn't want to hide from people anymore or run from every shadow.

Down on the surface, a man in a very expensive-looking suit left one of the hotels in the city and headed down the street towards one of the public vid com units.

The Pack plus two sat in the Tillar Palace. They had picked a table at the back looking out across the bar and into street. They were having a drink of coffee along with a sandwich and discussing what it was like to be in a band with Tate and Kato when Datch's vid com beeped.

He fetched it out and looked at it. It was from the spaceport saying that the Raven was ready to be collected and listed the repairs.

"That's the spaceport. The Raven is fixed and ready for collection."

"How much?" asked Fred.

"Thirty-two Thousand, five hundred and eighty-seven credits."

"Ouch."

"They did mount the two anti-aircraft missile systems. Wait, two?"

"Timbo. You didn't by any chance get another anti-aircraft system, did you?"

"Yes, I got one to replace the one that they mounted on the ship."

"Err… I think you need to get another now as they have mounted that one as well."

"They did?"

"Yes, sorry."

Timbo didn't look happy.

"Timbo. Look, why don't I buy you a nice new one as soon as I can do so without them trying to mount it on the ship."

"That would be very good Datch. Thank you."

He looked a bit happier now.

"Clax do you and Fred want to come with me to the spaceport to check out the Raven."

"Sure."

"If you guys stop here and watch to see if Dirk appears. We shouldn't be gone long."

"We'll call you if he turns up." Said Kato.

"OK."

With that the three of them got up and headed off to the spaceport to check out the Raven's repairs.

The man in the suit reached the vid com units and placed the prepaid card in the unit. It bleeped and he manually entered the user ID.

Up on the space station Dirks extra vid com beeped and started showing anonymous call incoming. Dirk breathed a sigh of relief.

"Hello?" he said.

"Do you have the merchandise?

"Yes, I have it with me. Do you have the credits?"

"Yes. All untraceable as we arranged. Meet me in an hour at the Tillar Palace as per your instructions."

"Ok. I'm on my way."

The call ended and he got up and headed for his ship.


Down below, Datch, Clax and Fred arrived at the spaceport and walk over to the service desk.

"Hi, we are here to check out the Raven. We needed some repairs doing and have been notified they are complete."

"And you are who sir?"

"I am the owner, Datch Thome."

She pressed a button and the unit scanned Datch's ID.

"Ok sir. The cost is thirty-two Thousand, five hundred and eighty-seven credits."

"No Problem."

"I will call the supervisor to go through the repairs with you. Please note: All repairs have a two thousand standard solar hours guaranty. Excluding damage from external sources."

"That's great, thank you."

"If you wish to wait over there. He will be with you shortly."

"Thanks again."

They walked over to some seats that the receptionist had pointed at and sat down.

Up above, Dirk powered up his ship and launched from the space station, heading towards the surface. He was watching his sensors, making sure nothing black was following him. He hit the outer atmosphere, and the ship's shields started to glow with plasma. Down below was the city and the spaceport. He did a quick scan of the other ships in the vicinity. Nothing! He contacted the spaceport and joined a line of the other ships going into land.

A man came walking over to Datch and stopped.

"Good afternoon, sir. If you could come with me, I'll take you to your ship and you can inspect the repairs."

"Thank you." Datch said.

They stood up and followed him through a door and down a corridor to the service area. They emerged into the daylight and there was the Raven with all of its holes repaired. Also, there were two new pods, one sitting on either side of her belly.

The supervisor stopped in front of the ramp leading into her cargo bay.

"We have repaired the damage to the hull and mounted the two missile turrets here and here." He said pointing to the pods.

"They gave us a little bit of trouble as we had to find a secure mounting point but they are both now linked into the ships weapons system. The rear pulse canon needed a new energy conduit fitting and the tactical system had been disconnected when the energy conduit had ruptured."

"How is the interspace drive?"

"We had to replace part of the gravitational stabiliser system as there was a big hole in one of them. Oh, and three of the shield emitters had big holes in them."

"Anything else?"

"We recalibrated the navigational array, refuelled it and cleaned your cockpit windows."

"Cool."

"If you would like to follow me, I'll show you the new missile interface and you can do a full system's check before approving the payment."

"Thank you."

They followed him inside the Raven.

Behind them a ship came into land in the main landing area. Onboard was Dirk. He shut the engines down and put on his disguise before leaving the ship to head for the rendezvous.

The supervisor took them to the cockpit and waited while Datch and Clax went through the systems checks and verified the systems were all ok. Then he called the spaceport.

"Control, we are about to bring the weapons online to demonstrate the additions."

"Copy that service."

"Right, if you instruct the ship to activate the weapons systems but with the safety locks on, please."

"Raven, please activate the weapon system but keep the safety locks active."

"Warning! The weapons systems will not be able to fire with the locks active."

"Understood. Please proceed with the activation of the weapon systems."

"Please note, addition weapon systems found: Two interspace missile platforms found."

Clax put his headset on and pressed a couple of virtual buttons.

"Hey, these are pretty good. They fire missiles that can chase a ship using a tiny interspace engine that locks onto the target ships interspace field."

"Does that mean we can shoot pirates down from a long way away?" asked Fred.

"No, they need to be close enough for the system to detect their interspace field which is about four hundred kilometres looking at this. But they look really cool."

Clax pressed a few more virtual buttons and then took his headset off.

"Raven, shutdown the weapon systems and deactivate the safety locks." said Datch.

"Weapon systems have shut down and will function normally upon reactivation."

"Raven, what is the status of tactical."

"Tactical systems are fully operational and long-range scans can be initialised."

"Raven, are all system operating at normal parameters?"

"All systems are operating at 100%"

"Cool."

Datch turned to the supervisor.

"Looks good."

"If you are happy with the repairs, please can you authorise payment." He said.

Datch looked across at Clax and he nodded.

The supervisor pressed some buttons on his vid com and a box appeared in Datch's mind. Datch confirmed the transaction and the box disappeared.

"You did include the tip for the work crew?" asked Datch.

"Yes sir. As you requested."

"Good. Thank them for us for all their efforts."

"I will sir. I shall leave you to your ship."

"Thank you."

The supervisor got up and Clax escorted him to the exit before heading back to cockpit.

"So, let's do a system scan and see if Dirk's ship is in the star system."

"Good call." Said Fred.

"Raven, initialise tactical scan for the ship we have be following."

The tactical plot started to appear and then a red circle started to flash on top of the Raven.

"Target located."

"Wow, that was fast." said Clax.

"Raven where is the pirate's ship?"

"The ship you are tracking is three hundred and fifty metres to the rear of the Raven."

"He's bloody here! Raven, is there anyone on board the ship" said Datch.

"Negative. The ship is unoccupied and its flight systems are shutdown."

He pulled out his Vid com and called Carina. Her image appeared on the display.

"Hi Datch. Everything OK?"

"Yes. Dirk is here in the city."

"How do you know?"

"Because his ships parked in the spaceport behind us."

"Oh, crap. I'll let Kato know."

"We're on our way too you."

"Raven, shutdown all the systems except for tactical. If the ship takes off track it as long as you can and notify me via my vid com."

"Affirmative. Shutting down all systems except for tactical."

They got up and hurried towards the cargo bay and the way out of the ship. The spaceport was very busy as they went through it enroute to the transit system checking the spaceport's concourse for Dirk on the way.

Five minutes later they were in a transit tube heading for the bar.

At the Tillar Palace the rest of the pack sat looking down the street for Dirk.

A man walked in and sat at a table near the front. He looked around nervously before ordering a beer. He took a drink and then scanned the bar.

Kato was looking out across the street when her sixth sense gave her a kick.

"Someone's watching me." she said.

"What do you mean?"

"I mean someone who knows me is watching me. I can feel it."

The rest of them started to look around the bar.

The man noticed them and looked out to the street before picking up his drink.

"Are you sure?" asked Carina.

"Yes."

The man finished his drink and stood up to leave. He turned and gave them a glance before leaving the bar and heading over to the public vid com units in the street. He typed in a message and sent it.

"Over there." said Tate.

Kato looked across. She took an image with her implant and then started checking it against people she knew.

It took a few moments and then she found the image she was looking for.

"I can't be sure, but I think he's part of the royal court. One the princess's aids." she said.

"It's a bit strange him happening to be here at the same time as Dirk." Added Tish.

"Do you think he could be working with Dirk?" Asked Krissy.

"Hmm. It would explain why the Princess thought we were dead."

"Ok. That's a bit too much of a coincidence thinking about it. Tate, you stay here with these guys and I'll follow him and see where he goes."

"I'll come with you." said Krissy who was very keen to help.

"Me too." added Rosey.

"Girl power!" said Krissy and everyone looked at her puzzled by what she had said.

"Err. It's an Earth thing. Sorry."

"Earth as in soil?" asked Tate.

Krissy looked blank for a moment.

"Sorry, Sol three." She added.

They shrugged their shoulders.

"Ok, come on."

They got up and headed out onto the street trying to keep a low profile. Which considering both Rosey and Krissy were wearing brightly coloured tops on a planet that didn't do bright anything's, it was going to be a challenge.

The man was a good distance ahead and just about to turn down a side street. They held back a bit and waited until he turned the corner before running up to the corner and stopped peering around it. The man was looking back every few moments.

"Has he seen us?" Asked Krissy.

"No, I don't think so. He's just checking to see if he's being followed, I think."

"He's not very good at it." Added Rosey.

"At this point I think that's a good thing." Said Krissy.

He reached another junction and turned right.

"Ok, come on." Said Kato.

They hurried to the next junction and looked down the street. This was quite a long street with shops on both sides.

"We'll have to follow him down here. The next junction is too far away and we could lose him. Try to make it look like we're out shopping."

"That should be easy." Said Krissy grinning.

"Yes, we're good at shopping." Added Rosey.

Dirk was on the transit tube system when he got a message on his vid com. He fetched out of his pocket and looked at it.

'Mr Dirk. I believe the princess's bodyguards are at the Tillar Palace so I'm moving the venue to Star city. Please meet me in the bar with the merchandise as soon as possible.'

Dirk was now very worried. If the bodyguards were here, the black ship would be here also and with it the rest of them. He looked around nervously. The plan was starting to go wrong but there was no turning back now. Still if he went to the space station he would see if they came after him. Also, inside the station the ship would not be transmitting its ID. He had changed the ID for the clean one that he used in the more policed parts of the galaxy but he suspected they had that as well as his normal somewhat tarnished one.

The pod arrived at the Tillar Place stop. He pressed a button on the control panel telling it to carry on to the next stop.

Kato watched as the man carried on down the road and around the corner. He was starting to relax a bit and had stopped looking around quite so much. They picked up the pace again to avoid losing him.

Dirks pod arrived at the next stop and after a quick look around he left the pod and headed down the street to Star city.

Star City was a two-story building with bright lights that lit up the front of it. It was a place for off-worlders, with a restaurant section upstairs that served a mixed cuisine of planetary and alien meals. Downstairs was set out with tables and chairs down the sides, along with taller tables and high stools in the centre. There were a number of large vid screens mounted at various places around the room, displaying various sports channels. A bar ran across the back wall, with stools in front of it. On the wall behind the bar was a very big mirror that ran the full length of the bar.

Dirk walked in and went over to the bar. He ordered a beer and sat down on one of the bar stools to wait for the courier to come in. He sat watching the mirror carefully, that way he could see who came into the bar without being noticed.

Datch, Clax and Fred arrived at the Tillar Palace and went over to the rest of the Pack.

"Hi folks. any sign of him?"

"No, none at all." Said Carina.

"In fact, the bar seems to have thinned out a bit now." said Peebop.

"Must have been lunch time when we came in."

"So, what's the plan now?" Asked Hagger.

"Well, he should have been here by now if he was coming. He was not at his ship when we left the spaceport. What's happening with Kato."

"She suspects one of the royal court is involved, we spotted him standing at the bar. He noticed us looking at him and left. Kato is following him with Rosey and Krissy."

Datch got out his vid com and called Rosey.

"Hey Datch. What's up?" she said appearing on the screen.

"We know Dirk is in the city. But so far, he's not shown up here. Where are you folks?"

"We're about three blocks away. Somewhere near to the next transit station, I think. There is sign pointing up the road to it."

"I wonder if they spotted, Kato or Tate. Let me know if he goes in a bar."

"Ok Datch."

He closed the call.

"What are you thinking?" Asked Fred.

"I think that the guy from the court was here to meet Dirk. He spotted Kato or Tate and moved the meeting place."

"They will want to meet somewhere with a lot of people so they can blend in with crowd and easily disappear afterwards." said Tate.

"Hmm."

They sat thinking about it.

Meanwhile, three blocks away the man turned left at the next junction and disappeared down the street. Kato, Rosey and Krissy headed towards the corner but keeping a bit of distance.

Just down the road was Star city. The man looked up and down the street before walking inside. Dirk spotted him and put his hand up. The man came walking over and sat down on the stool next to him.

"Dirk?"

"Yes."

"Nice disguise."

"Thank you."

"Can I see the merchandise?"

Dirk moved a small bag along the bar towards the other man. He opened it and took out the Jackar to inspect it.

"Do you have the credits?"

"Yes."

The man removed a small data cube from his pocket and slid it along the bar to Dirk.

"As we agreed. Ten million credits in untraceable data packets. Her ladyship and our friends are very grateful to you. Thanks to you they will soon be able to return home. I take it, you are going a very long way away?"

"Thank you and yes. I plan to move to the other side of the galaxy."

"Good. No offence but please try to stay there."

The man picked up the small bag and put it in his pocket.

"Good day, Dirk. Enjoy your drink."

"Good day, sir."

The man got up and headed to the bathroom leaving Dirk sitting at the bar.

Kato, Rosey and Krissy came around the corner.

"Can you see him?" asked Kato.

"No." said Rosey.

"Me neither." Added Krissy.

They looked up and down the street. The man had vanished.

"Look! Do you think he's in there?" said Krissy pointing down the street to Star city.

"I bet he is. Come on." Said Kato.

They headed down the street to the bar and stopped outside.

Dirk looked up and spotted them in the mirror. He froze as he was lifting his drink and started watching them intently.

"Do you see him?" said Rosey.

"No. Do you think he went upstairs?"

"We had better have a look."

They walked inside and headed to the stairs.

Just then the door from the toilets opened and the other man came out. Dirk waved at him and pointed up the stairs. The man nodded and went back in the toilet.

The three of them came back down the stairs and went back outside.

"He must have gone in another bar. Let's try the one over there." Said Kato.

"I'll call Datch and let him know what's going on." Said Krissy.

Back inside Star city Dirk breathed a sigh of relief as he watched them head off down the road. He waited until they had gone and then went to the toilet to fetch the other man.

"Thanks, I would have walked right into them. Which way did they go?"

"They went that way, down the street and you're welcome." He said pointing.

"Ok, I'll go the other way to the transit."

The man left the bar checking up and down the road first before hurrying up the street towards the transit stop.

Dirk turned back to his drink. There was no point downing it. They had looked straight at him and not recognised him. This old man's disguise made him look about two thousand years old with a grey beard and moustache along with the hat which had a feather in it and thick padded coat. He looked so completely different; his own mother wouldn't have recognised him.

Datch along with the rest of the Pack finished their drinks and then headed to meet up with Kato, Krissy and Rosey. The trip on the transit system took about 3 minutes and soon the pod was pulling into the next stop.

"I'll call Krissy and tell them to meet us outside Star city."

"Yes, sounds good and if need to we can fan out into the surrounding bars." Added Tate.

On the opposite platform a man watched them as they arrived. He didn't like public transport but this was the safest way to travel as lots of people meant you could stay hidden in the crowd. He hurried up and entered a pod that would take him back to his hotel. Then he could head back to Thoth as fast as possible.

Datch and The Pack stepped off the Transit stop and headed down the road towards Star City. The street was quite busy with people milling about, in and out of the shops. There was also a number of café's, bars and restaurants mixed in. All of them were very busy and doing a lot of trade. Datch stopped and waited outside Star City, his eyes scanning the crowd for any sign of Dirk.

Dirk looked up from his drink. 'hmm' he thought 'it might be time to move.' There was an outside chance someone might spot him. He finished his drink and picked up his cane that was leaning against the bar. He decided to go for the theatrical approach and started to hobble across the bar. As he approached the doors. Datch started to head inside with the rest of The Pack. Datch opened the door and then waited while and old man came out.

Dirks heart was pounding in his chest and he was starting to sweat. He hobbled past Datch and the rest of The Pack and then just to complete the masquerade said 'Thank you, young man' in a croaky voice before hobbling up the street towards the transit stop. As soon as he was out of their sight, he started to pick up the pace.

He reached the transit system and finally got into the safety of the pod. He fetched out a bag that he had in his pocket and started to remove the disguise placing it in the bag. He deflated the airbags in the lining of the coat and removed the wig on his head before sitting back to relax. He was a rich man now.

In Star city, The Pack got a round of drinks and sat down with Kato and Tate. They had just gone through all the bars twice along with the Café's, restaurants and the shops. There was no sign of either the member of the royal court or Dirk.

"I think they have given us the slip." Said Clax.

"I'll second that." Said Peebop.

"I don't think they are here anymore either. We would have seen them." Said Fred.

"Yes. I agree. They're gone alright." Said Kato.

"What now?" asked Krissy.

Datch looked thoughtful for a moment.

"Let's grab our things from the hotel and head back to the Raven. We know he'll go back to his ship at some point and if they have met up it will be sooner than later."

"We can't sit in the Raven at the spaceport." Said Clax.

"I know. We take the Raven and head to the edge of the star system and wait for him to launch."

"Then what." Asked Tate.

"Well, his friends put a few holes in us, so we return the favour. Disable his interspace drive so he has to return here. Then we ask the authorities to detain him for shooting at us."

"OK. sounds good. I still have my security ID so they should listen to us." Said Kato.

"OK, we have a plan."

They finished their drinks and headed back to the hotel.

They were just walking through doors of the hotel when Datch's vid com beeped. He took it out of his pocket and looked at it. It was a message from the Raven.

"Folks, we need to move it. Dirk has just powered up his ship."

"Datch, I'll grab our things, you head to the spaceport and start getting the Raven powered up." Said Carina.

"Ok! see you in a few minutes."

He turned and ran out the door towards the transit system.

Inside the hotel the Pack ran to their rooms to collect their bags. A few minutes later they were back in reception signing out. Once everyone was done, they also ran for the transit system.

Datch arrived at the spaceport. He went through security and headed to the Raven. It had taken him fourteen minutes to get here. He ran up the ramp into the Raven and headed straight to the cockpit.

"Raven, where is the target ship?" he said sliding into the pilot's seat.

"The target is enroute to orbit."

"Show me on the tactical," he said as he started powering up the ship's systems.

The plot appeared in the centre of the cockpit. There were a lot of other ships about, but Dirk's was lit up with a red circle. Datch watched it as it climbed up through the atmosphere and finally left it, reaching orbital height. The ship was not following the normal corridors for exiting the system. Instead, it was following the traffic heading to the space station. He watched as the ship slowed down and then entered the central core of the space station before stopping and shutting down its beacon. The little dot turned green, meaning the ship's systems had powered down.

Datch relaxed. That's why they hadn't seen it when they came into the system, with tactical down they were only able to see ships with active navigation beacons. He was on the station the whole time. It made sense when Datch thought about it. Why risk being on the planet when he could watch and wait in orbit until he needed to go to the meeting. That way it would be a very short trip to the surface of just a few minutes and when everything was completed a short trip back. Then, when he was ready to leave, launching from the station would be a lot safer as it would only be a matter of a minute or two before he could go to interspace.

Datch sat looking at the traffic going to and from the space station waiting for the others.

# To Catch a Dirk

Ten minutes later the rest of the Pack came running up the stairs and into the cockpit. Datch was sitting relaxing looking at the plot in front of him.

"Err Datch, where is he?" asked Clax sliding into the seat next to him.

"I suspect he's on the way to a bar to have a beer."

"A beer? What do you mean?"

"He's on the space station."

"You sure he's not just trying to lose us?" asked Carina.

"No. Not at the speed he was going. A cargo ship could have out run him going at half speed."

"Oh!"

"I've set up tactical to look for his ship's energy signature as well. So, if he changes ID's we'll still see him."

"So, what are we doing?"

"When everyone is ready, I think we need to check out the bars on the station."

"Why are you so sure he'll be in a bar?" asked Fred.

"Well, he came here for a reason and I suspect that the man from the royal court has now got the Jackar and our pirate friend is a very rich man."

"You mean they paid the ransom?"

"No, the King wouldn't do that. He would try to hunt him down." Said Kato.

"Yes, that can't be it." Added Tate.

"I'll contact the Princess and ask her. If nothing else she will need to know about the member of the royal court who was meeting with Dirk."

"OK, you do that. In the meantime, let's go see if we can catch a Dirk."

Datch turned to the front and finished going through the pre-flight checks and then brought the thrusters to standby.

"Tillar Control, this is Raven ready to launch on route to Star View station."

"Raven, lock on to beacon 32541, launch will be in two minutes thirty seconds. Hover at fifty metres and wait for beacon."

"Copy that control."

Datch increased power to the thrusters and the Raven left the ground. He then waited until the beacon turned green and then pointed the nose to the sky and headed up through the atmosphere. The journey was quite slow by normal flight speeds as the trip to the station had traffic that moved at slower speeds such as shuttles etc.

"Star view station, this is Raven on approach from Tillar city requesting docking in the central core."

"Raven, this is Star View control. You are number nineteen in the que. Please come to station keeping at two thousand metres on beacon SVS227 and wait for clearance."

"Copy that Star View. Heading to station keeping."

The Raven moved towards the station and then came to stop relative to the station. Two minutes later the comms burst into life.

"Raven, you are cleared for docking, head to bay twelve."

"Copy that. Bay twelve."

Datch matched the stations rotation and then moved toward the docking bays entrance. It was a large rectangular slot in the centre of the station with flashing lights around the edge.

Datch followed another ship inside. The interior was a cylinder with landing pads scattered all around the inside of it. Each had a number on it.

Datch spotted number twelve and slowly lowered the Raven down onto it with a slight bump as the ship contacted the pad. There was then a clunk as the pad's clamps took hold of the Raven's feet. The pad started to move downwards into the station. Datch started to shut the systems down and watched as they drop down the shaft. The lift slowed and then started to move to the side along a track to the landing bay where it came to a stop.

"OK, looks like we're here. Time to work out how we are going to do this." Said Clax.

"Well, first we need to work out the layout of the station and then I think we should split into two groups." Said Kato.

"Sounds like a plan. Let's find a café we can sit inside, less chance of him spotting us that way."

Datch put his headset down.

"Raven, keep tactical active and notify my vid com if the other ship powers up."

"Affirmative tactical will remain active."

They got up and left the ship.

The station was quite old and some of the corridors needed a coat of paint but it was clean and well lit. They walked up a blue and yellow corridor and came to a security check point. After being scanned to verify their IDs, they were let through into the main station.

The inside of the station was not an open space like most space stations but was built of different levels all on top of each other. Each had a number of large streets that ran from one end of the level to the other where lifts would carry the inhabitants to different parts of the station. Each large street had smaller ones leading off them that were lined with shops or living accommodation.

The Pack found a café that had enough seats to push together to make a large table. After rearranging the furniture and some very funny looks from the staff they sat down and took out a map of the station that Krissy had spotted on the way out of the security check point. They ordered coffees all around and then spread the map out across the table. Each level was colour coded along with all the shops, bars, restaurants and hotels. It made the map very colourful.

"OK, I think he's going to be in a bar or restaurant that has a view of the planet below." Said Datch.

"Why?"

"Well, I suspect that the man from the royal court told him we were on the planet so he will be watching for the Raven coming up."

"We just have!" said Fred.

"Yes, but how long has it taken us to get to here from the ship?"

"Err, about twenty minutes."

"If it took him the same amount of time plus say ten minutes to get to a bar and sit down. We would have been starting to dock by then and therefore he wouldn't have seen us coming up from the planet."

"Oh, so he's watching outside now in case we come to the station?" asked Krissy.

"Yes."

"How does that help us?" asked Tate.

"He'll be looking out of the window and not at the door to the bar. Also, it limits the number of bars that he will be in."

Datch looked at the map and started to point out serval of the bars that where on the lower level.

"These ones here look out towards the planet."

"Err, isn't the station rotating?" asked Krissy.

"Yes, but these bars are located on the sides of the external docking ring. That stays stationary so large liners can dock easily with the station."

"Oh, does that mean we have to go to the docking ports?"

"No. there are three sets of transit pods to take us to the public part of the docking ring."

"There are three access points?" asked Kato.

"Yes, three."

"Hmm, we may have to split into three groups in case he tries to make a run for it. We don't want to lose him."

"Can you ask the station security to help?" Asked Fred.

"I can try. I've still got my royal security ID."

"I'll come with you." Said Tate.

"You folks wait here and we'll go to the security office."

Kato and Tate headed off to ask if the security services could hold his ship until they located him as he was wanted for a crime against the royal family.

It took about half an hour before they returned.

"What took you so long?" Fred asked.

"They've agreed to hold the ship, but they said they need to scan him before they'll release him and the ship to us. We also asked if they could help us find him, but they said we'll have to apprehend him ourselves as they don't have the manpower to search the station for a petty thief."

"Oh. Okay, let's head down to the docking ring and start looking for him."

The Pack got up and headed to the lifts. They had already decided that Datch, Carina, Krissy, and Peebop would go with Kato in the first group. Rosey, Hagger, and Fred would go with Tate in the second group. Then Tish, Dapo, Tank, and Clax would be with Timbo in the third group.

When they reached the bottom level, they split up and headed off to the three docking ring access points. These were similar to lifts, but they moved along the direction of travel of the docking ring. They would match the speed of the station's rotation or slow down to a stop to match the docking ring. The docking ring had its own artificial gravity systems, so the transition from the gravity of the main station to the docking ring was seamless.

The plan was to work their way around to the next team's starting point. That way, they hoped they would find him.


Dirk was sitting looking out of a window. The scene outside was quite relaxing, with ships coming up from the planet with cargo and passengers while others were heading down to the surface. Most were the standard white colour to make them easily spotted if they needed rescuing. There were also a few that were brightly coloured, and some that looked like they could do with a wash, but more to the point, none were black!

He took another sip of his beer and ordered a steak dinner. Another few hours and he would start the six-month trip towards the galactic centre before heading out towards the far side of the galaxy. He had spotted a nice, quiet star system that he could make his home, and after a few years of chilling, he could get himself a new ship and start his own legitimate shipping company. "To hell with this part of the universe," he thought to himself and picked up his drink.

A little way up the corridor and on the opposite side of the docking ring, Rosey, Hagger, Fred, and Tate came out of the transfer lift.

"Which way?" Rosey asked.

"This way, I think," Tate said.

They walked along the corridor and spotted a bar.

"Okay, if he's in there and tries to make a run for it, let me grab him. If he pulls a weapon, dive for cover. I mean, dive for cover as well. I don't want you getting shot."

"We don't want to get shot either," Fred said.

"But what if he gets away?" Hagger asked.

"He won't. His ship is being held, and if he pulls a weapon, he won't get off the station. The security services will stop him. Okay, are we ready?"

They all nodded. Tate walked through the doors, followed by the others.

It was quite a large bar, but narrow, with most of the seating running along next to the windows. The view looked out towards the star, which was shining through the windows. But even here, its light was quite low compared to other stars, and it was orange in colour. Thousands of stars filled the rest of the view, surrounding the star's orange glare.

They walked slowly down the bar, casually looking at the customers, before heading back the other way and finally out the door.

"Well, he's not in there and I have a feeling we are on the wrong side."

"Wrong side?" Asked Rosey.

"Yes, we should be able to see the planet, not the star."

"I did wonder where that was." Said Hagger.

"Ok, there must be a crossover point somewhere up here."

They started to head up the corridor, looking for the way through to the other side. There were a few shops, and Rosey decided to do a quick check inside them, just in case Dirk had decided to get a new wardrobe to disguise himself. She came out with a number of new tops, as she said it would be rude not to.

It was a few hundred metres before they found a corridor leading to the other side. They made their way across to the planet side of the ring. Just up the corridor was a bar and restaurant.

They went inside the bar and started to look around. Sure enough, the view out of the windows was now of the planet, and ships could be seen coming and going from the station. Above their heads was a star liner docked to one of the ports. The outer hull of the station could also be seen out of windows, and was rotating below them with an almost hypnotic effect.

The inside of the bar was laid out with seats all around the edge, and had a circular bar in the centre of the room. It was quite busy, with a lot of people sitting and having food, and others propping up the bar and drinking. They started to work their way through the tables, looking for Dirk.

Fred spotted someone near the window that looked similar to Dirks picture and called the other. They started to make their way towards him splitting into two groups.

Dirk finished his steak. Now, did he fancy another drink. Yes, he thought. Then he felt a cold shiver run down his spine.

Tate had almost reach him when the man turned round.

Dirk turned around and put his hand up to attract a waiter.

Tate stopped.

"Err, can I help you, mam?" asked the man looking at her.

"Oh, sorry to disturb you sir. Is everything ok for you. We're part of the quality department just doing a random check."

"Oh, yes, very good thank you."

"Have you eaten?"

"Yes, I had the Altaren stew. It was very nice."

"Has the service been good."

"Yes, everything was very good."

"That's great. Thank you for your feedback. Please enjoy the rest of your day."

She turned and walked away. The four of them waited until they had gotten back across the bar before saying anything.

"That was close," Fred said. "I thought it was him."

"He did look similar, that's for sure," Tate said. "Okay, next bar."

A waiter came over to Dirk and took his drink order. As he went away, Dirk looked to his left where the star liner was docked a bit further down the ring and wondered if it would be better to take that. No, he thought, he didn't want to leave any loose ends behind, so he had to take his ship. He could get rid of it later or even re-register it under a new name. Hmm, no. A bigger ship would be better. After all, he had enough credits to get a small, second-hand freighter if he part-exchanged his ship. Just then, the waiter came back with his drink.

"Thank you," he said.

"You're welcome, Sir. Do you require anything else?"

"No, That's all thanks."

The waiter headed back to the bar leaving Dirk with his thoughts.

Tate's group headed into the next bar along. It was a relaxing kind of bar, with an artist playing a synthesizer in the corner. After having a good look around for Dirk, they decided to contact the others. Kato's group was behind them, and Timbo's team was in front of them - or a very long way behind, which was a little mind-bending until you realised that they were working their way around a loop. Tate told Kato which bars they had been in, and Timbo told them the name of the bar they had started in.

There was a chance they could miss him, but as the security services were holding his ship, they would notify Kato if he tried to go back to it.

They moved on to the next bar.

Kato's team, with Datch, Carina, Krissy, and Peebop, walked into the next bar. This one was quite colourful, with bright lights and a stage. They walked over to the bar and decided that, as this was the fourth bar they had been in, they should have a drink of Gruck. While Peebop and Krissy ordered the drinks, the rest of them had a walk around the bar to check if Dirk was there. He wasn't.

They walked over to the others at the bar.

"Well, no sign of him here," said Datch as he approached Peebop.

"Oh. How many more do we have before we get to where the others started?" he asked as he passed Datch his drink.

Datch pulled out his vid com and put up a list of the bars around the docking ring. He looked at it closely before turning back to the others.

"I think we have three more before we reach the crossover point," he said.

"Well, let's hope he's here, as it will take forever to search the rest of the station," said Kato.

They all took a sip of their drinks and looked around again.

"If we find him and he starts to run, just trip him up, okay? I'll do the rest." added Kato.

"Okay."

Datch went and stood between Krissy and Carina. He put his arms around both of them. Krissy looked thoughtful for a moment, and then stepped a little closer to let him get his arm properly around her. He smiled, and then realised that he didn't have a spare arm for his drink. He pondered the problem for a few moments, before giving up and taking his arm from around Krissy and picking up his drink.

"Err, I need another arm," he said quietly.

Carina looked at him for a moment.

"No, just a really long straw," she said.

Both she and Krissy laughed. Peebop turned to look at them, and Datch went a bit pink.

"What did I miss?"

"Err, nothing," said Carina.

When they had finished their drinks, Kato turned to them all.

"Okay, let's move to the next bar," she said.

They made their way to the next bar. They couldn't see outside the windows in this one, as there was a very large starliner blocking the view. The lack of the view seemed to have reduced the population of the bar by quite a large amount, as it was almost empty. They had a quick look around, but there weren't many people to check.

The next bar, however, was very busy, and they split up into two groups to work their way through it. There was a great view outside the windows of the side of the starliner. It looked to be about five hundred meters long and three hundred meters high. It had two large interspace engines at the rear, and Datch could just about make out a dome on the top.

Datch, Carina, and Krissy headed over to the far end of the bar and started to walk back to the bar slowly, casually checking the tables as they went. They had gotten about halfway across when Datch's vid-com beeped.

He stopped and looked at it. It was a message from Tish.

'We've finished the bars in our section and are walking back towards you via the shops on the opposite side. We'll meet you at the crossover point. Tish.'

Datch sent back 'OK, we've one more after this one. Datch.'

They'd just about got back to the others when Datch's vid-com beeped again.

This time it was Rosey saying they'd finished and were heading towards them.

"Looks like we're last," said Datch to the others.

"We are?" asked Krissy.

"Yeah, the others are heading to our last bar."

"I hope we haven't missed him. It's going to be a right pain in the neck searching the rest of the station," said Peebop.

They did another quick look about before heading to the last bar.


Dirk finished his drink and got up and headed to the toilet. He was feeling full and was starting to relax now. He figured the black ship must still be on the surface. They must be hunting the bars down there for him. He smiled to himself and walked through the toilet door.


Datch's group came walking into the last bar. It was another big bar and was also busy. It had large windows that looked out to the planet below and, just to the left, was a starliner. They decided to split up again and headed to either end before walking slowly back to the bar, checking as they went. They had just arrived back at the bar as Tate, Rosey, Haggar, and Fred came walking in through the doors.

"Hi guys. Any luck?" asked Datch as they came walking up.

"No, you?" asked Fred.

"No. I think we must have missed him. The others will be here soon. We'll have a drink while we wait for them, then we'll have to come up with plan B."

They turned to face the bar and started to order their drinks.

Dirk walked out of the toilet and started to walk across the Bar towards the door. Krissy picked up her drink and turned to look across the bar at the scene out of the window. Dirk spotted them as she turned around and started to run for door.

"He's there!" she yelled.

Tate and Kato turned and started to sprint after him.

He made it out of the bar into the corridor. He had a good ten-metre lead on them and pounded up the corridor, and then turned into the crossing point. Tate and Kato had to slow down when a couple of people walked out of the shop next to the bar. Dirk was starting to think he was going to get away when he came out of the other side of the crossing point. He turned to look back to see where they were and then came to a sudden stop. He went to move back and two arms grabbed him like a giant vice. He looked up and then up some more into a face with a very evil grin on it. He swallowed hard.

"Mr Dirk. My friends would like a word with you about a number of holes in our ship and a couple of pairs of soiled underwear!" said a voice that put another set of underwear in severe danger.

Dirk wayed up his options and came to the conclusion that he currently didn't have any.

Tate and Kato arrived followed shortly after by the rest of them.

"Well done, Timbo. Looks like you caught a Dirk." Said Kato.

"What we going to do with him now?"

"We take him to the security office so he can be scanned."

"Err, any chance of letting me breath?" Asked Dirk gasping for beath. He was starting to go a funny colour.

"Hmm, can they scan him when he's unconscious?" asked Hagger.

"I'm not sure, but I think they would prefer him awake." said Kato.

"Ok. Dirk do not give Timbo a reason to put you to sleep because he will really enjoy doing it." said Tate.

Dirk nodded, he had gone very red.

Timbo slowly released his grip and Tate got out some handcuffs and put them on him.

"What are you going do with me?" he said as soon as he was able to talk.

"That depends on how cooperative you are. We're going take you to the security services where they'll scan you about the meeting you had with the member of the royal court and the handing over of the Jackar."

"If I don't own up?", Timbo started to frown, "Just asking!"

"Timbo here will have a quiet word with you in a soundproof room."

"Oh."

"Right, let's get him to the security office." Said Kato.

"Yeah, the sooner we get this sorted, the better." Added Tish.

They made their way to the transfer pod, and then headed to the nearest security office.

They arrived outside the security office without any issues as Tate and Kato were on either side of Dirk and Timbo was right behind him. There was zero chance of him escaping other than maybe by killing himself.

"Alright folks, we'll take it from here. You go and get yourselves a drink. It'll take a while to process the information. I'll message you when they're done." Said Kato.

"Alright, we'll head back to the bar where we found him and wait." Said Datch.

Tate and Kato took him inside and The Pack headed back to the bar.

Kato walked up to the desk and the officer behind it looked at them and then at Dirk.

"Good afternoon, officer. I am Kato of the royal security services from the Thoth star system. This man is wanted in connection of the theft of Princess Zafira's Jackar. We have already arranged with your main office to have him scanned and then handed back to us for transport to Thoth."

"Please wait a moment while I check the details."

The officer looked at the vid on the desk and pressed a few buttons. It beeped and he looked up.

"OK, that checks out, would you like follow me please."

"Certainly officer."

They gave Dirk a prod and he followed the officer through the door at the back. The officer took him into a room with another officer and Dirk was placed in a chair with an antenna apparatus above it.

Dirk looked at the machine. Soon they would know everything and there was nothing he could do to stop them.

The officer turned to Kato.

"How long ago to you want to go back?

"We think the Jackar was handed over about two hours ago so, let's go with the last three hours."

"Ok. If you could wait in there, I'll call you when we have extracted the information." He gestured to the room opposite.

They went in and sat down.

The Pack arrived at the bar and found some tables that were close together and sat down. They ordered a round of drinks and started to wind down a bit.

Datch sat next to Krissy and Carina sat on the other side of her.

Datch turned to Krissy and whispered in her ear.

"So, me and Carina were wondering if you'd thought about what we talked about?"

She looked at them both.

"Yeah, I have, and the answer is yes, I want to give it a go. But I need it to go slowly. This is all new to me and I found it hard when I just had a boyfriend back on Earth, so having both of you will take some getting my head around."

"Okay, we'll take it nice and slowly then." Said Carina.

Datch smile at her and gave her a kiss on the lips and then Carina did the same.

Dapo happened to be looking across at them and then he turned to Tish.

"Did you just see that?" Asked Dapo.

"What?" Asked Tish.

"Datch just kissed Krissy in front of Carina and then Carina kissed her."

"Are you sure?"

"Yes."

"Maybe they are doing some sort of Sol three thing."

They both looked over at them.

The waiter came over and brought their drinks. Datch picked up his beer and took a big swig, then sat back in his chair. Carina was busy showing Krissy something on her vid com.

"Well, they're not doing anything now. Maybe they were just being friendly, they do live together."

"Hmm, maybe."

They carried on drinking.

Carina was showing Krissy other groups of people who were in polyfidelity relationships. They were all famous, of course, or they wouldn't be in the public eye.

"Yes, but I'm a bit worried about the sex thing with three of us." Krissy said quietly.

Carina smiled.

"You don't need to be; we don't all have to have sex at the same time. Yes, it would be nice every now and again, but I won't have a problem if you and Datch sleep together, and the same goes for Datch if me and you did. We did talk about it before we asked you."

"Oh, okay. Maybe the three of us can go through things together. I know our biology is similar, but it still worries me a bit."

"Look, here's what I'll do. When we get back on the Raven, you and I can go to your room and I'll run through some basics with you, okay?"

Krissy smiled.

"Yes, that would be great."

Datch had gotten up and gone over to Fred, who had been staring into space. It turned out that he was trying to think of a good title for a new song.

"Fred, are you okay?" Datch asked.

"Yeah. We always do a song about our adventures, so I thought I would try and think of one." Fred said, snapping back into reality.

"What have you come up with so far?"

"Well, I have 'The Chase', 'Pirates in the Dark', or maybe 'Rebels without Hope'."

"Hmm. I like the last one."

"Yeah, but are we the rebels?" Clax asked, who had been listening.

"Hmm. Good point. We'll have to think about that."

In the security office Kato and Tate were viewing the memory download. The officer confirmed that the recording showed the Jackar being transferred, and the conversation between Dirk and the member of the royal court pointed to the theft. The security services agreed to hand Dirk and his ship over to Kato and Tate, as well as a copy of the download.

After searching Dirk, they found the data cubes with the credits on and handed them to Kato. They would keep Dirk in custody until they were ready to leave.

They finished watching the replay and thanked the officer for his help. They left the office, leaving Dirk in the hands of the security services.

As they were walking back, Kato turned to Tate.

"Is it me, or are we missing something?"

"I know what you mean. The member of the court said 'Her ladyship and our friends.'"

"It must be someone who has been banished at some point. But how would the king abdicating enable them to come home? If the princess takes the throne, I doubt if she would pardon anyone, surely?"

"Hmm, it would be very dangerous to do so, that's for sure."

They continued to the bar. When they arrived, they got a beer and went over to sit with The Pack.

"So, did he have it?" Datch asked as they sat down.

"Yes, the scan showed the meeting with the man from the royal court and the Jackar being handed over."

"Cool, was he in one of the bars?" Fred asked.

"Yes, he even walked right past us."

"What? I didn't see him." Datch said.

"You even held the door for him. He was the old man that came out the door as we were going into Star City."

"Wow, that was a good disguise." Carina said.

"There are a few things that don't add up. One, the conversation with the member of the court, and two, his friends on the pirate planet."

"Why don't you contact the Princess and see if she knows anything?" Rosey suggested.

"Hmm, not at the moment. I'm starting to get a very bad feeling about this." Tate said.

"Yes, the pirates were very organized, almost too well."

"They baited us when we followed him from the base. The ships that attacked us were more like fighters than pirate ships."

"Yes, and he talked about 'her ladyship?'"

"Who is she?"

"Hmm, we don't know. But I suspect she's someone with a lot of power." Tate said.

"I think we need to have a talk with Dirk on the ship after we leave the system. I know it's not your thing, but Timbo, could we borrow you for a little while?" Kato added.

"Err, I'm not into hurting people, just putting them to sleep. But maybe with him, a little bit more would be fine. He did have our ship shot at."

"Well, what about holding him upside down for a bit?"

"I can do that and maybe even bounce him up and down a bit as well." Timbo said, starting to grin. It was like watching the jaws of death showing its teeth.

"I think the grin should do it." Hagger said.

"Okay, should we go?" Datch asked.

"No, let him stew a bit. The security services have said they will hold him until we're ready to leave. They're also transferring him to the main security suite near the landing bays for easy transfer to our ship. So, let's have some food and take our time. The longer we wait, the more likely he is to talk."

"Can't you just scan him?" Tish asked.

"Yes, but only when we get back to Thoth. The courts here may not grant the scan straight away. It could take weeks before they agree, and by then the King will have stepped down. I want to know what's going on before that happens."

"Hmm. I see your point." Datch said.

"I think I will send a message to the King's security team telling them what we know and that the Jackar has been handed over to a member of the royal court."

"Won't they tell everyone?"

"No, if I know them, they will start watching people very closely and see who does something out of character."

"Okay. I think it's time for a bite to eat. So, who wants what?" Fred asked.

"I think I'll have the stew." Dapo said, grinning.

The Pack settled down to have a very long and relaxing lunch.

# Treachery

The Pack had just finished a very nice steak dinner with all the trimmings, but the station did not have ice cream. This was a little disappointing, but they decided to have some in the ship on the way to Thoth.

The flight to Thoth would take eight hours, as Dirk's ship could only travel at interspace twelve. That was the fastest they had seen it go, anyway. Tate would pilot it, while Kato and Timbo took care of Dirk. The rest of them would follow in the Raven.

Kato turned to Tate. "I'm going to contact one of my friends in the King's royal guard and see what he knows."

"Why the King's guards?"

"Well, the more I think about it, the more I'm convinced the traitor is in the Princess's court. They knew she was with us and our route, and the Princess seemed to know a lot more than she should. Things don't seem to be adding up."

"Well, hopefully Dirk will give us some answers."

Kato turned to The Pack. "Are you about ready, folks?"

"Yes, I think so," said Datch, getting up.

They all finished their drinks and headed off towards the security suite where Dirk was being held. It was only two hundred meters from the bay where his ship was. They arrived at the security office, and an officer went to fetch him from the cells.

Kato turned to The Pack. "Okay, folks, he's going to try to engage you in conversation and then try to talk his way out of it. So, don't listen to a word he says. Ninety-nine percent of it will be lies, and the rest will be adjusted to make you feel sorry for him."

"Also, try to avoid eye contact. He will be looking for someone to focus on. That is, apart from you, Timbo." Added Tate.

"Me?" asked Timbo.

"Yes, you just grin at him. It will unnerve him." Said Kato.

"Okay." Said Timbo, who then proceeded to put on the evilest grin he could think of and would have made even the most seasoned space pirate run for the bathroom.

"Everyone okay?" said Kato.

They all nodded.

"Datch, I'll put his ship on dual band transmission," said Tate. "I'll use band D channel 997 to talk with you, and I'll keep the comms channel open. That way, if he does try anything, you'll hear it."

"Okay. No problem. What do we do if he gets control of the ship?"

"He won't, but if he does, take out the engines. I'll be flying in front of you to make it easy for you."

"Okay."

"I mean it! Do not hesitate. That's all he will need. Okay?"

"Okay."

The officer came walking back with Dirk in front of him. He stopped in front of Kato.

"If you would accept the custody of the criminal, I can release him to you."

"Yes, officer." She waited for a box to appear in her head and then accepted it.

"We have also overridden his ships controls and given both your IDs control of the vessel."

"Okay. Thank you for all your help in this matter."

"Just doing our job, ma'am."

"Well, thank you on behalf of Thoth."

Dirk was pushed towards Kato. She grabbed the handcuffs and started to lead him out of the office.

"Err, where are you taking me?" Dirk asked.

"You're going to Thoth to stand charges of theft and treason against the crown."

"I won't let you have the data, and without that you can't do a thing."

"On Thoth, if you do not give up the data, it is considered as guilt and as good as saying you did it. So, you lose! Now move it!"

They moved down the corridor towards the landing bays. Dirk's ship was a few bays away from the Raven. They arrived at the one with his ship in and stood outside of it while Tate went onboard and locked Dirk out of the systems. That way, he couldn't cause any problems while onboard. After a few moments, she signalled Kato to tell her everything was good. Kato and Timbo then took Dirk onboard, while the rest of The Pack headed to the Raven.

Datch sat down in the pilot's seat on the Raven. He put on his headset and switched the comms unit to dual band.

"Tate?"

"Yes, Datch, I hear you."

"Cool. Everything okay?"

"Yes, he is with Kato and Timbo and apparently being very quiet. If you launch first and hold just outside the station perimeter, we'll come to you after launch. That way we can both jump to interspace together."

"Okay, copy that."

He opened a channel to the station.

"Star view Station, this is Raven ready for launch on route to Thoth."

"Raven, launch will be in two minutes. Prepare for lift. Ten seconds."

The bay floor started to rotate and then moved along a short corridor into the elevator. The pad along with the Raven started to ascend to the launch area. Datch watched as the wall of the lift shaft scrolled down in front of him. After a few moments, the lift slowed down and then the Raven surfaced into the landing and departure area.

"Raven, automated launch in forty-five seconds. Lock on to beacon SVS 771."

Datch pressed a couple of virtual buttons.

"Star view station, Beacon Locked on and ready for launch."

The thrusters started to fire and then the main engines increased power. The Raven started to move forwards. Around them, other ships were taking off and forming into a line ready for station exit. The Raven followed a large freighter out of the station exit and into space.

"Raven, beacon will release in thirty seconds."

"Copy that Star View Station. We will be holding for another vessel before going to interspace."

"Raven, hold on beacon SVS119H."

Datch waited until he had control and then moved the Raven to the holding beacon.

Star View Station, Raven is on the holding beacon."

"Raven, interspace is at your discretion. Please instruct the second vessel to request holding beacon SVS119H."

"Copy that Star View Station."

Datch pressed a virtual coms button.

"Tate?"

"Yes, Datch?"

"We're on holding beacon SVS119H. If you request it when launching, it should bring you to us."

"Thanks, Datch. Requesting launch now."

Tate started the ship's systems and requested launch. The ship was very old, and half of the systems had warning lights on them. She thumped one of the panels, and several warning lights went off. She came to the conclusion that either the systems had started working correctly or the warning lights had just given up. One way or another, the lights had gone off.

"Computer, what is interspace status?"

"Interspace Drive is s s s operating a a at seventy-two percent."

She sighed.

"Computer, run a diagnostic on your voice unit, please."

Outside, the lift started to move.

"Star Queen, lock on to beacon SVS794 for launch and then to beacon SVS119H when clear of station."

"Copy that, Star View Station."

"Diagnostic checks complete. Delay in neural net detected. Rerouting." Said the computer.

The ship reached the top of the lift and sat waiting for clearance.

The Star Queen started to move. It was a slow departure, and it took six minutes to clear the station exit. Tate turned the ship and headed to SVS119H. The Raven sat there waiting in space.

Datch watched as the Star Queen came up alongside. The Star Queen was a very battered-looking ship, with the tip of its right wing looking as if someone had recently replaced it and then forgotten to paint it. Datch was now hoping he didn't have to shoot at it, because looking at it, one shot would likely mean they would be picking everyone up from space.

"Datch?"

"Yes, Tate?"

"Are you ready?"

"One sec. Raven, set course for Thoth, interspace twelve. Keep within firing distance of the Star Queen."

"Course laid in. Do you wish weapons to be enabled?"

"Yes, but lock on to engines only."

"Weapons enabled and Star Queen's engines have been selected."

"Okay, engage drive when the Star Queen jumps to interspace."

"Confirmed."

"Okay, Tate. We're good over here?"

"Okay, Datch. Going to interspace."

The Star Queen jumped to interspace, and the Raven followed behind. The stars flickered as the two ships sped through space.

On the Star Queen, Kato got up from her seat and walked over to where Dirk was sitting with Timbo. Timbo stood up.

"What are you doing?" Dirk asked, looking nervous.

"Well, that depends on you," Kato said. "We are in deep space now, and no one can hear you scream."

"What do you mean?"

"If you tell me who 'her ladyship' is and who the other people are, then we'll get you a nice drink and you will have a pleasant flight."

"You know I can't tell you who they are. They would kill me."

"Hmm, I thought you would say that. Timbo, if you could please give Dirk a different perspective."

Timbo grabbed hold of Dirk's legs and hoisted them into the air. Dirk's body followed, banging his head on the floor in the process.

"Ouch! That hurt!"

"I will ask you again. Who is 'her ladyship'?"

"If you think hanging me upside down will make me talk, it won't."

"Timbo, have you ever heard the term 'not big enough to swing a cat'?"

Timbo looked into space for a moment.

"I have now." He said and grinned.

"Well, let's see if this cargo bay is big enough to swing a Dirk."

"I'll hit the walls."

"Quite possibly."

Timbo started to turn in a circle, and Dirk's head started to get closer and closer to the walls. He still had his hands handcuffed together behind his back.

Timbo increased speed, and Dirk's head was just missing the wall, with bits of his hair catching various bits of equipment as he went round. Here and there a few strands of hair would get left behind, with an "ouch" or two from Dirk. At the speed he was being flung around, it would hurt a lot if his head hit the wall.

"Should I let go?" asked Timbo.

"Should he, Dirk?"

"He wouldn't dare." Dirk said as he passed Kato.

"Timbo."

Timbo let go with one hand, and one of Dirk's legs started to flop about.

"No, NO!" said Dirk.

"Are you going to tell me?" asked Kato.

"Err…"

"Timbo, Let go."

"NO! Wait! Wait! It's the Princess!"

"Timbo, put Mr Dirk down."

Timbo slowed down and dropped Dirk to the ground with a large bump.

"What do you mean, 'the Princess'?"

"She will kill me for telling you."

"Go on."

"The theft was staged so it would then cause the king to abdicate."

"Yes, but you had the Jackar."

"The Princess didn't want it with her in case someone found it. I was paid to take it to Klayton and give it to one of her aids. Then you guys made me change plans and I had to detour to the base."

"Who were the 'pirates' that shot at us?"

"They are not pirates; they were part of the royal guard until they got expelled for plotting against the King. The Princess is going to bring them back in return for backing her."

Kato looked at him thoughtfully for a moment. It did make sense, and she knew about the attempted coup a few years previous. It would also explain why the Princess thought they were dead. She must be in contact with the rebel forces, and they told her about the fighters that chased after them.

"Why should I believe you?"

"I'm a dead man now, either way. If it's not the truth, then I'll be executed, but if it is and the Princess finds out then I'm also dead."

"Are you meant to be joining the rebels?"

"No, I'm meant to be heading to the far side of the galaxy and never coming back."

"Hmm. Timbo, go and get Mr Dirk a drink. I need to go and make some calls. Mr Dirk, do not try anything stupid. There is another ship following this one and its weapons are locked on to the engines. Any sign of trouble and it will remove your engines. Also, Timbo here will not be happy with you and will remove one of your arms or legs."

Dirk looked at Timbo.

Timbo walked back across the room with a cup of water. He handed it to Dirk and grinned. Kato waited until Timbo was sitting opposite Dirk.

"Timbo. If he even twitches the wrong way you can hit him."

"It will be my pleasure, Kato."

Kato then headed to the cockpit.

Tate sat watching the stars fold in front of the ship as it moved ever closer to Thoth.

"Did he confess?"

"More than that. He explained what's going on and it's the Princess, she's after the throne."

"What?!"

"She wants to be queen and if the king has a male heir, she'll lose her chance. She also has some rebel guards helping her."

"Are you sure?"

"Not totally, but it does make sense. The lack of information from her about what was going on, the member of the royal court who was helping her, and the pirate ships that were more like fighters than raiding ships."

"Oh, so what do we do?"

"I'm going to call my friends in the royal guard. They need to know what's going on. Hopefully they can come up with a plan."

"Do you think they can stop the abdication?"

"I don't know. But we have to try."

"Datch, did you hear that?"

"Some of it, can you say it again."

Datch and Clax sat listening to Kato repeat what she had said to Tate. Afterwards, Datch spoke.

"What do we do now?" he asked.

"Put your tactical sensors online and look for any ships that have a signature similar to the ships that attacked us. If you see them, contact us immediately."

"Ok. I'll do that."

Datch turned to Clax.

"Bloody Jaxx," he said.

"Well, that's a surprise," said Clax.

"Yes, just a bit. She fooled us well and truly."

Datch pressed the ship's comms.

"Guys, we have some news for you. Maybe you should come up here."

Back on the Star Queen, Kato put a call through to one of her friends. The call lasted quite a while, during which she was transferred to a commander who listened to her and noted the details. Finally, the call ended.

"What did they say?"

"They are looking into it and are going to try and delay the abdication without alerting the Princess. It is due to take place in four hours. If they can delay it, it will give us time to get there with Dirk."

"OK, but that is, as long as Dirk lets them download all the data concerning the plot?"

"He will, I think. He's trying to save his neck. Once they have the data, they can arrest the Princess and the abdication will be cancelled."

As the two ships got closer to Thoth, the Raven's tactical sensors started to signal a warning. Datch looked at it.

"Tate? We have company."

"What?"

"It looks like ten ships similar to the ones that shot at us."

"Where?"

"They are sitting in space near the edge of Thoth space."

"I expect they will be waiting for the abdication. If they went in now, they would be shot at."

"One thing though, our course is going to take us quite close to them."

"How close?"

"About six million miles."

"You mean they will see us?"

"Yes."

"How long?"

"Hmm, twenty minutes maybe."

"Thanks. I'll contact our friends."

"Clax, I think we can stop targeting the Star Queen and start thinking about the ships that are about to chase us."

Clax pressed a few buttons and put his headset on. Datch turned to the others who had come up to the cockpit.

"Buckle up folks, this could get bumpy."

"Datch, I have spoken to our friends and they are sending fighters but we're going to have to go it alone until we get to them."

"Copy that."

The two ships reached the edge of Thoth space and went past the waiting ships. Onboard the leader of the rebel ships shouted down the comms channel.

"That's Dirk's ship and the Black one. They must have captured him. We need to stop them from getting to the planet!"

All ten ships headed towards them.

"Looks like they're coming folks," said Datch.

"Copy that. I've got the engines maxed out!" said Tate.

"Clax, see if you can get a target lock on the lead ship with the missiles."

"It's still too far away."

"When you get a lock, fire! Don't wait for them."

"OK."

The ships behind started to close on the Raven.

"How long?"

"About twenty seconds."

Then there was a gentle kick from the underbelly of the Raven and a missile streaked out the back before vanishing. It then reappeared in front of the lead ship, detonating on its shields. Clax let another go. This time when it reappeared, it flew into the ship and took half of the wing off. The craft went tumbling and spiralling out of control into the darkness of space.

A second ship took its place and fired its forward cannons. Two blots of green plasma sped through space towards the Raven, hitting the rear shields, but due to the long range, the plasma just dissipated into nothing.

Datch had positioned the Raven between the fighters and the Star Queen to give it some protection.

Clax fired another missile and the second ship's shields lit up. The fighters started to back off a bit, realizing that the missiles had a limited range, but they continued firing plasma bolts. Then they spread out into a long line.

"What are they doing?" asked Datch.

"They're going to come at us all at once, I think," said Clax. "That way they can hit us hard and we may only get one or two of them before we're gone."

"I'm not having that," said Datch. "Get ready to fire everything you've got. Tate, get that ship to Thoth!"

Datch pulled back hard on the stick, turning at the same time. He hit interspace factor seventeen for a second, and then spun the ship downwards. This had the effect of the Raven starting to go up, disappearing, and then appearing above and slightly behind the fighters.

Clax opened fire as Datch pushed the Raven into a dive towards the fighters. Flames erupted from fighter after fighter as the Raven flew through the middle of them, opening fire with missiles and cannons. The fighters couldn't respond, as their weapons all pointed forwards and the Raven was on top of them before they could turn.

"That pilot's a madman!" yelled the leader, as his shield took a direct hit, disabling it. Around him, six ships exploded in flames.

Datch pulled up and hit interspace seventeen again, disappearing before appearing behind the Star Queen again.

"Let's not do that again!" said Hagger, looking very green.

Datch looked behind the Raven. The fighters were trying to regroup, but pieces of exploding ships were not helping their navigation. Finally, they managed to form up into a small wing of five ships. Now things were a little more even.

In front of the Star Queen, another fighter wing of twelve ships appeared. This time they were heading straight towards them.

"Datch, follow me through. They're on our side," said Tate.

"No problem," said Datch.

The comms burst into life.

"Kato, you and your friends head to the planet. There's another fighter wing waiting to escort you down. We'll take care of these ones."

The fighters flew right past them, heading for the enemy fighters. The attackers spotted them and split up, turning tail and heading out of the system.

Ahead of the Raven was Thoth and another fighter wing. The Star Queen slowed down, as did the Raven.

"Datch, shut your weapons down. We're good," said Tate.

Clax powered down the weapons systems.

Another voice came on the comms.

"Kato. We are to escort you to the palace landing area. The King's security commander is waiting there for you."

"Thank you," came Kato's voice.

"Don't thank us yet. There is a fight going on at the palace. Some of the guards are holding the king and princess captive."

"Why?"

"They heard the abdication had been postponed and are demanding it continues."

"How many?"

"About twenty of them, we think. Anyway, follow us down."

The group of ships started to descend towards the planet through an empty sky. There were no other ships, as the spaceport had been locked down. Below them lay the capital city, with the palace next to it. There were a lot of troops and vehicles surrounding the palace, and a number of fighters circling it. Smoke was coming from one of the windows, and the occasional blast of plasma fire could be seen coming from some of the rooms.

The fighters stayed airborne while The Star Queen and Raven landed in the landing area. A ship the size of the large freighter was sitting with its doors open, and a lot of troops were coming and going.

"You folks stay here. I'll find out what's going on," said Datch, getting up.

"I'll come with you," said Dapo.

"Okay, Carina, can Dapo borrow your pistol?"

"Yes, it's in our room with yours."

"Okay, come on."

Dapo got up and followed Datch out of the cockpit.

When they came down the ramp, they were greeted by two guards and Tate.

"Hi, Tate," said Datch.

"Hi. Where are the others?"

"They're staying onboard the Raven for now, in case things escalate and we need to get out of here."

"Okay, no problem. Follow me over to the command ship. Kato's already there with Timbo and Dirk."

Datch and Dapo followed Tate over to the other ship. They walked up the ramp and into a large room with tactical displays in the centre and a number of officers manning them. At the far end, a man in a commander's uniform sat with Kato and Timbo.

Tate led them over to him and saluted.

"Ah, Tate," he said. "Glad to see you. Kato has just been bringing me up to speed on what has been going on. You must be Datch."

"Yes, sir. This is my friend Dapo. We were the two who went to the Princess's aid on Starlight station."

"Yes, I have read the report that Kato sent to us. You are a very resourceful bunch of people."

"Thank you, sir."

"We have a bit of an issue here at the moment, as you can see. They are holding the princess and the king hostage and demanding that the king abdicates. They have also put up a dampening field that could stop the transport of their brains if they kill them."

"Sir, I don't think the princess is a hostage. From what we know, she is the one running the show," said Kato.

"Hmm, yes, but how can we prove that without getting the king killed in the process?"

"What about the Jackar?" asked Datch.

"She'll have it back by now," said Kato.

"Yes, but how does she know it's hers?"

"Dirk gave it to the aid. I'm sure she will have checked it."

"What if Dirk had given her a copy?"

"She wouldn't be able to take the throne until she had the real one back."

"I like your thinking, Datch," said the commander.

"Err, one thing though, she has it and we don't," said Kato.

"We can make another one in the Raven's replicator."

"Yes, but how do we make her believe that she has a fake one and we have the real one?" said Tate.

"Dirk! We get him to help us."

"Err... He's guilty of treason. Why would he help?"

"What about we offer him what he wants?"

"What?"

"He wants a fresh start on the other side of the galaxy. So, we let him go on the understanding that he never comes back and helps us free the king."

"Hmm," said the commander thoughtfully. "Kato, what do you think?"

"I'm not sure, sir. I don't trust him."

"Tate?"

"Well, sir, we're sort of running out of time, so I think it's worth a try."

"Okay, it goes against the grain a bit, but I'm willing to give it a go if Dirk will do it. It will give us a distraction if nothing else. Kato, go and fetch him please."

Kato headed off to fetch Dirk. A few moments later, she came back with him in handcuffs.

The commander looked him up and down and then said, "Mr. Dirk, today is your lucky day."

Dirk looked at him. When people tell you it's your lucky day, it normally isn't.

"Is it?" he asked.

"We want you to help us free the King," the commander said.

"Err, you do?"

"Yes."

"And what do I get?"

"What you wanted all along, Mr. Dirk. If we free the King and you give us all the memories concerned with the Jackar and the deal involving the princess, you can take the princess's credits and leave with the understanding that you'll never come back here again."

Dirk thought about it. Given his current situation, it sounded like a good deal, considering that the other options were prison, prison followed by death, or even prison followed by death followed by more prison.

"So, I go free?"

"Yes. We will escort you to the edge of our space and point you in the right direction."

"Hmm. OK. Deal."

"Deal."

"So, what do I have to do?"

"I take it you have a way of contacting the person who took the Jackar?"

"I have an emergency contact, yes."

"Well, contact him and tell him that you have the real Jackar and the one you gave them was a fake one. Tell them that you want another ten million credits for it or you're going to go public with the whole deal."

"The princess will want to kill me."

"Yes, at all costs, because if it gets out, it will stop any chance of her taking the throne."

"But how will that help?"

"Her allies are overstretched as it is, and if they see things are unravelling, they will drop support for her and make a run for it. Then we can arrest her."

"Have you ever thought of becoming a master criminal? You would be very good at it." Dirk replied.

"I'm not sure whether I should take that as a compliment or have you shot." said the commander.

Dirk shut up in case it was the latter.

"Right, let's put this plan in action. Kato, you go with Datch and sort out the fake Jackar. I'll set up what looks like a break in our forces, that way they will think they have a way out."

Datch and Kato headed back to the Raven and into the engine room.

Kato pulled up images of the princess's Jackar from the planet's database and then added a chip to one of its arms where it had gotten knocked when the princess was younger. She also added the royal seal that was on the underside that no one knew about apart from the inner court.

They were watching the replicator build it when Carina came in.

"Hey, what are you two up to?" she asked.

"We're cooking up a surprise for the princess," said Datch with a grin.

"Can the rest of us help?"

"No babes, we're good. Tell the others to chill in the rec room for a bit."

"Are we safe?"

"Yes, I think so at the moment."

The replicator finished what it was doing, and the result was a small, round pot made of gold with arms and legs. It had a small face on the front and the top was in the shape of a pointy hat that was welded on.

"What is inside?" asked Carina.

"It is the Princess's essence taken from her birthing fluids." Said Kato.

"Ewe. I wish I hadn't asked."

"It is a very private part of our culture and we believe Jackars keep our souls for us."

"Wow. I take it, that is empty?"

"Yes."

"We're good" Said Datch picking up the Jackar.

"Ok, let's get back to command." Said Kato.

"Sorry babes, but we need to go."

"OK, you keep your head down."

"I will."

Carina watched as Datch and Kato headed down the ramp and trotted over to the command ship. She then went back and told the others what Datch had said.

Datch and Kato walked in with the Jackar and went over to the commander.

"That looks very good he said looking at the little figure. Right, Mr Dirk. Show time."

Dirk was given back his vid com.

"Err, I need to be in a bar, not a command ship when I make the call or they will know it's a trick."

"Yes, but I'm not going to allow you to go to the city."

"What about the Raven's cargo bay?"

"That's not a bar."

"It can be. It's got an array of holo emitters, we can turn it into a bar."

"Hmm, it may work. But what bar."

"The one on Star View Station. I can download my memories of it to the Raven's computer. It should be able to recreate it."

"That sounds promising. Lieutenant, go with Kato and accompany Mr Dirk to the Raven, we wouldn't want him getting lost on the way. Oh, and Timbo. Thank you for your help in these matters and if you would like to go back with Datch, please do."

"Thank you, Sir."

# Jackar or Jackar?

They headed back across to the Raven and stood in the cargo hold.

Datch stood in front of the computer terminal and pressed a few buttons. Then downloaded his memories of the bar to it.

"Raven, please us the file that I have just downloaded to create a holo graphic replica of the bar using the cargo bay emitters."

"Please wait. Processing."

The cargo bay slowly turned into a busy bar. It had just about finish when Carina and Krissy came walking in.

"Are we having a party?" asked Carina.

Datch turned to look at them.

"Err, no, just setting the scene to make a call."

"Well, you missed a few bits." Said Krissy.

They looked around and there were a few black bits with no detail or showing the cargo bays wall. One of the missing bits was smack bang in the centre of the window.

"Hmm. Do you two remember what the bar looked like on the station?" asked Datch.

"I do, I was recording everything in case it got exciting." Said Krissy.

"Cool, do you remember how we showed you to download the recordings to your vid com?"

"Yes."

"Ok, go over to the terminal there and download it to the ship."

"Ok."

"Raven, Krissy is about to download a file to the cargo bay's terminal. Please use it to enhance the images from the holo emitters in the cargo bay."

Krissy pressed a button and waited.

"Okay, done." she said.

"Please wait while the processing completes." said Raven.

The holes in the holographic bar started to disappear. When the processing was finished, they looked around.

"Well, it looks okay, but let's see if it runs. Computer, run the simulation." said Datch.

The bar came to life. People were chatting, drinking, and eating. Through the window, ships could be seen leaving and approaching the station. A waiter went from the bar delivering drinks to a table. It all looked very real.

"Raven, how long until the holo repeat plays?"

"The current playback length is eighteen minutes and forty-two seconds."

"That should do it."

Kato turned to Dirk.

"Are you all set?"

"As ready as I can be. Any chance of a drink for a prop? I'll go to that table over there."

"Sure, anything to make it work better."

"I'll get it." said Carina and disappeared for a few moments.

She came back with a glass of brown liquid and gave it to Dirk. He took a sip.

"This is just coloured water."

"If you don't like it, I'll call over our waiter, Timbo."

"No, this will be fine."

"Okay, it's time to make the call."

"Datch, restart the holo playback."

"Raven, restart the holographic playback."

The bar jumped back to the start position and started to play again.

"Dirk."

He picked up his vid com and pressed some keys.

It took a few moments, but then a man's face appeared on the screen.

"Why are you calling me?" he asked in a somewhat annoyed tone.

"Well, I've been doing a bit of thinking, and I want more credits," Dirk said, picking up the drink and taking a sip.

"You were paid for the job, and we have the Jackar, so our business is complete," the man said.

"Yes, but one, you don't have the Jackar, I do. And two, from what I can see on the news channels, things are not quite working to your plan. I wonder what would happen if I went to the press with what I know. I wonder how much they would pay me?"

"What? I don't believe you."

Dirk lifted up the copy of the Jackar and showed it to the vid com, making sure the man spotted the chip and the royal seal.

"What? How?"

"I'm a very good forger. Even the weight is exactly the same."

"How much do you want?"

"Twenty million."

"Well, you're going to have to wait until the Princess takes the throne."

"Oh no, no, no. I want to be long gone by then. I don't want you sending men after me. Twenty million will get me a new identity and a whole new life a long way from here."

"We are having a few issues at the moment. So, we might have trouble getting it to you."

"You have four hours. I'll call with the drop location then. If not, I'm contacting the press."

Dirk dropped the call.

"How was that?" he asked.

"It should have done the trick. We'll go back and inform the commander," Kato said.

Kato, Datch, the Lieutenant, and Dirk headed back to the command ship.

In the palace, the aide went to the Princess, who was talking to one of the rebels.

"Err, sorry to interrupt, but we have a problem, ma'am."

"That is an understatement."

"No, another problem."

"What?"

"The Jackar Dirk gave you is a fake. He has the real one and is threatening to go to the press with it unless he gets twenty million credits."

"What! We checked it."

The Princess started to pace up and down, her face turning red.

"Yes, but apparently, he is a very good forger. He even made it the same weight. We will only know by removing some of the fluid and testing the DNA in it."

"Well, do it!"

"We can't. The facilities to do it are external to the palace."

"He'll have to wait. Tell him."

"He won't. He's given us four hours or he goes to the press."

"Well, let him."

"Your Highness, if he goes to the press, you will never be able to take the throne."

"What? Just kill him."

"We can't. Everyone is either here or in space fighting for their lives! They tried to shoot down the black ship and came under heavy fire. The Imperial fleet has now engaged them."

"You're telling me that our ships couldn't take down one ship with a rock band in it? I'll have their lives for their incompetence."

"Your Highness, the ship they have is not normal. It destroyed the two fighters we sent after them, and now the Imperial fleet is involved."

"I don't care! Make it happen! I order you!" she screamed.

The two rebels looked at each other. This was not how things were meant to go. The Princess was losing her head. She had promised them a royal pardon and a homecoming as heroes. Not death threats. One turned to the other and whispered,

"I think we need an escape plan. Tell the others to see if they can find a way out."

The other man nodded and left the room.

Down the corridor, there were a number of men with a plasma cannon, taking pot shots at the royal guard through an open window.

"How are things looking?"

"It looks like they're planning a frontal assault, sir."

There was a loud thud as the cannon fired, hitting the shields protecting the royal guard. They fizzed with energy as they absorbed the plasma bolt. Two more plasma bolts came back, hitting the palace shields and causing plaster to fall from the ceiling close to the cannon.

"Men, see if you can see a way out. Her ladyship won't be able to take the throne. Dirk still has the Jackar. Pass it on to the other men."

"Are we taking her ladyship with us?"

"Hmm, I would say that's in the balance. But we need a way out."

He turned and headed back to the room with the Princess.

Down the corridor, the King was locked in a room with one of his aides. He could hear his daughter shouting about something but couldn't hear what. It was turning out to be a very bad day for him. He had been put into a tight corner and had no choice but to abdicate. He was about to do so when his aide had received a call telling him to wait as the royal security services were getting information about a possible plot. He had called a stop to things while waiting for more information. What happened next was a lot of gunfire, and he and his daughter were taken hostage. He and his aide were placed in one room, and his daughter and her aides were placed in one down the corridor.

The princess was still pacing up and down the room, shouting, "I hate him! I want him dead! I'm the queen, he must die!"

The other man returned to the room.

"Commander, order your men in space to find Dirk and kill him."

The princess was red in the face and looking very angry.

The commander walked over to the console in the corner of the room and the other man shook his head.

"Sorry, ma'am. I can't."

"Why?"

"Because they have all been destroyed."

"What, all of them?"

"Yes, ma'am."

"Well, send some of your men outside to find him."

"Your highness, we are barely holding the palace as it is. We don't have anyone to spare."

"But I need him dead!" she screamed.

"Janger and I will take care of it personally."

He nodded to the other man and they headed out the room.

"Are you mad?" said Janger.

"No. We're leaving. I don't care about her ladyship anymore. She's lost it. We need to get out of here and fast."

"Yes, but where to?"

"We'll get back to the ship and head to the base at Garhar. We can work out where to go from there. This part of the galaxy is not going to be a good place for us."

They arrived at the plasma cannon.

"How's it looking?" the rebel commander asked.

"It looks like we may be able to get out over that way. They have pulled most of the troops around to the front of the palace ready for a frontal assault."

"Okay. Set the cannons on automatic firing and head down the stairs over there. We'll wait there for the rest. Janger, you go fetch the others."

"Yes, sir."

"Men, follow me."

The commander headed to the stairs with the men, while Janger went to fetch the others.

The princess was standing, looking out of the window.

"What is going on?"

The aide was standing at the consoles, looking at the screens.

"It looks like they are getting ready to attack. Our people have moved more cannons to the front, so we should be secure."

"Good. As soon as Dirk is killed, I can take the throne."

"What about the king?"

"He can have a stay in the cellar for a bit, and when I've consolidated my rule, we'll put daddy on an island somewhere to live."

"Yes, ma'am."

Janger reached the other men.

"Come on, guys. The boss said we're getting the hell out of here."

"What about the princess?" asked one of the men.

"No, Chancer. She's staying. The princess can't win, but is refusing to accept it. We've spotted a weakness on one of the sides where the royal forces are spread thinly. We think they are building up for an assault at the front. Set the cannons on auto and follow me."

They went along to the row of cannons, setting them up before heading back to the stairwell.

At the command ship, one of the officers called across to the commander.

"Sir. The rebel cannons have adopted an automatic firing pattern."

He turned to Kato.

"It looks like our little ruse may be working."

"Yes, sir."

"Lieutenant. Watch the right side of the palace for movement. If you see a group of men coming out, let them get past our lines and let the squad we pulled back know."

"Yes, sir."

The rebels all met up in the bottom of the stairwell.

"Men, the princess has lost her mind, and we're getting the hell out of here before the shit really hits the fan," said the rebel commander.

He opened the door and checked to see if the coast was clear.

"If we head along the hedges to the edge of the grounds, using them as cover, we should be hidden pretty well. The royal guard will be focusing on the front, so they shouldn't spot us. Then we head up the hill to where the ship is hidden and get the hell out of here. Okay?"

"Yes, sir."

The group of men started to make their way along the hedge, keeping it between them and the royal forces. Unknown to them, a covert scanner was watching them from the rear of the palace.

"Sir, they're on the move," said the lieutenant.

"Is the princess with them?"

"No, sir."

"Good, let them go."

The rebels reached the edge of the palace grounds and looked around. The royal guard were mustering their forces towards the front of the palace, just as the rebel commander had thought.

"Okay, up there, follow that ditch and hurry," said the rebel commander.

The rebels started to head up the ditch, making use of any cover they could find.

"Sir, the rebels have left the palace grounds," said the lieutenant.

"Okay. Time to close the net. Order the troops to surround them."

The royal guard who had been mustering at the front now broke away from the main force and headed up the side of the palace, cutting off the rebels from it.

On the other side of the hill, a detachment of troopers lay in wait, hidden in the bushes near the rebels' ship.

The rebel commander looked back towards the palace and spotted the troopers coming after them.

"Move it, men! Looks like they've seen us."

They hurried up over the hill and dropped down again towards the ship. They followed a narrow lane with tall hedges on both sides. The track was gravel, and they kicked up some dust as they headed towards the ship.

They reached the bottom of the hill and came into the clearing where the ship was parked.

"We're almost there, guys."

They started to pick up pace, but as they crossed the clear area, the bushes around them came to life. They walked straight into the waiting clutches of the other troopers.

"Drop your weapons!" shouted the lead trooper.

The rebel commander looked around him. They were surrounded by forty troopers, all pointing their guns at them. They didn't have a chance.

"Men, drop your weapons," he said.

The rebels dropped their weapons, and the troopers took them into custody.

"Sir, we have captured the rebels," said the lieutenant.

"Good. Focus our weapons on the cannon on the right-hand side."

"Yes, sir."

The pounding switched to a single point. The shield started to weaken, and plaster started falling from the ceiling in the room where the princess was.

"What's going on?" she shouted.

The aid ran out the door to find the men. Down the corridor, the plasma cannon was firing by itself. He ran to the other cannons. No sign of the men. He turned and ran back to the princess.

He took a deep breath and walked through the door.

"Your highness, the men have left us."

"WHAT?!"

"They have gone, your highness."

" THE COWARDS!"

"Your highness, what do we do?"

The princess stopped and thought for a moment.

"Take the consoles out into the corridor and then come back in and lock the door. They will think we were held captive too."

The aid moved the consoles out into the corridor and put them near the cannon. He then headed back to the room, locking the doors as he came in.

"All done, your highness."

"Okay. When they come to us, bang on the door. Then, when things quiet down, you can get a hit man to take out Dirk before he tells the press everything."

"What about the rebels?"

"They won't say anything. They have as much to lose as I do."

"Okay, ma'am."

There was a loud explosion in the corridor as the shields finally gave way. Outside, the troopers rushed in through the door the rebels had exited from and up the stairs. They ran to the other plasma cannons, shutting them down and securing the palace. The shields were shut down, and the troopers checked room after room.

They found the room with the king and shouted through the door.

"Your majesty, please wait until the techs get here. We need to scan for booby traps," the lead trooper shouted.

"Okay." a voice came back through the door.

Back in the command ship, the commander got up.

"Well, Kato, Tate, shall we take a walk?"

They followed him outside to a waiting transport before going to the palace. The main doors were opened, and they went in. Ahead of them, a team of techs with scanners checked the corridors for booby traps.

They arrived at the king's room, and the tech scanning the door nodded to the commander.

The lead trooper blasted the lock off, and the doors flew open.

The commander walked in.

"Your Majesty, are you okay?"

"Yes, is my daughter okay?"

"Yes, your Majesty, but we need to talk to you before we free her."

"Why?"

"Let's just say, your Majesty, that things are not as they seem."

"Please, tell me, Commander."

The commander and Kato went on to explain what was going on, and then Dirk was sent for and questioned by the king. Dirk explained how the princess had given him the bag during the theft and how the other man had thought it was a normal robbery. Dirk had waited until they heard someone coming to do it. He then pretended to mug her, pushing her to the floor, so it looked good. He went on to explain about the rebel base and the aid that paid him for the services.

The commander then explained how Dirk had helped them and the deal they had done.

"Well, that's quite a story. I take it you have all the memory downloads to back it up?"

"Yes, your Majesty. They have all been downloaded and verified."

"Hmm, is my daughter still locked in the room?"

"Yes, your Majesty."

"Okay, let's go and see what she has to say for herself."

The commander led the king down the corridor past what was left of the plasma cannon to the room with the princess inside it.

"Mr. Dirk, Kato, please wait here until I call for you." said the king.

"Yes, your Majesty," said Kato.

"Commander, if you could do the honours, please."

The commander nodded to a trooper who had been given a spare key for the door.

He turned the key and opened the doors.

The king walked in, followed by the commander and six troopers.

"Daddy, Daddy, you're safe! Those horrible men wouldn't let me come to you. I was so scared."

She ran across the room and gave the king a hug. He looked down at her.

"Did they hurt you?" he asked.

"Yes, they slapped me and pushed me into a chair."

"Hmm. Is there anything else you would like to tell me?"

The princess looked at him for a moment. Something wasn't right, so she put on her innocent face.

"No, why?"

"Kato, would you like to bring our friend in?"

"What?" said the princess, looking worried.

Kato walked through the door with Dirk.

"That's the man who took my JACKAR!" she shouted.

"We have his memory downloads. You planned all this from the start," said the commander.

"I'M GOING TO KILL YOU!" she shouted and started to run at Dirk.

The king stopped her and pushed her towards two of the troopers.

"Restrain her, please," said the king.

"Dirk, when I become queen, you are a dead man!"

Her aid started to move towards the door. The commander nodded at two more of the troopers. They grabbed him.

"What? I had nothing to do with it!" he said.

"Memories do not lie," said the commander. "Take him for scanning."

"What? Wait, no, no, I'll tell everything!"

He was taken out of the room, still protesting.

The king turned to his daughter.

"Well, my daughter, you will not become queen. I will make sure of that."

"But daddy, I can change. I really can."

"No, you won't! Commander, please take my daughter to a cell fitting for her treachery. I shall decide what is to be done with her later.

The princess was marched out of the room. The king let out a sigh as they left and turned to the others.

"Kato, I misjudged you earlier. Thank you for all that you have done."

"Thank you, your Majesty, but it wasn't just me. Tate and The Pack helped, and I wouldn't have been able to do it without them."

The king looked thoughtful for a moment.

"These were the people who brought you and the princess back?"

"Yes, your Majesty."

"Hmm, well, tell them they are invited to dinner with me tonight." He stopped for a moment. "And I know it's a break in protocol, but I would like you, Tate, the commander, to join me as well."

"Thank you, your majesty."

"Err," said Dirk.

"Err, what? Mr. Dirk, you are lucky to be getting out of a very long and painful prison term."

"Nothing, sir. Thank you, your Majesty." he said.

"Commander, please make sure Mr. Dirk's ship is refuelled and he leaves the Thoth system as soon as possible."

"Yes, your Majesty."

"Mr. Dirk, if you ever return to this system again, you will be spending a very long time in a very dark cell. Do you understand?"

"Yes, your Majesty."

"Troopers, please escort Mr. Dirk to his ship. He is to stay there until he leaves our system."

The two troopers saluted and motioned to Dirk to move into the corridor. Dirk left with the troopers, leaving the king with his aid, Kato, and the commander.

"Kato, please go and inform Tate and, err, The Pack?"

"Yes, The Pack, your majesty."

"The Pack, that they are invited to come to dinner this evening. Say 8pm."

"Yes, your Majesty." Kato turned and headed out of the room.

"And commander, please can you fill me in about what has happened before I make a planetary address?"

"Yes, your Majesty. I shall need a few minutes to deal with the rebels, and then I'll give you a full report."

"Thank you. Oh, and make sure their cells are very uncomfortable."

"Yes, your Majesty." He saluted and left the room.

The king sighed and replayed the memories from Dirk using his implant. They were very hard to watch. His own daughter betraying him. He sat down in a chair with a tear in his eye. He sighed again. It was time to have a male heir, maybe two. She was not suitable to rule.

# Dinner Guests

Back at the Raven, Datch was sitting in the cargo bay having a beer with Krissy and Carina. The others were watching a film in the rec room. Datch had told the Raven to keep repeating the bar's holographic projection as he liked the idea of having a large bar to hang out in. They had also got some chairs and a table to sit at from the replicator as the holographic ones were very hard to sit on. The holographic bar reminded him of the Barber's Inn back home.

The three of them were sitting around the table, discussing things. Krissy was a bit worried about the whole three-way relationship thing.

"I know you two are used to seeing people in, um, multi-person relationships," said Krissy.

"Yes, multi-person," said Carina.

"But what happens if it doesn't work out?"

"Worst case, whoever isn't working out will move out. But that's not going to happen. Even if you decide you only want to be intimate with Datch, we'll still be close friends." said Carina.

"Yes, and the same goes if you end up liking Carina more. It won't change the rest of the relationship. The key to multi-person relationships is to make sure everyone is aware of what's going on so that no one gets jealous or hurt. That way, the friendships can still work." Added Datch.

"So, sort of like friends with benefits?"

"Hmm, yes. It means we can all have fun together and also enjoy the sexual side of things when we're in the mood."

"You mean if I'm in the mood and Datch is busy, but you're not, then that's okay?"

"Yes, the same goes for each of us. The sex is an added bonus. I think we're already close in terms of our relationship."

Krissy thought about it. They had taken her in and made her feel like part of the family. She was very comfortable living with them They had become very close over the last year. No wait, it was two Earth year since she arrived on Bellatrix.

"Are you okay?" Carina asked, noticing the look on her face.

"Yes, I just realized, it's been two years since you brought me to Bellatrix."

"Wow, is it that long? That's flown by," Datch said, taking a sip of beer.

"Hmm, I don't want to have to move out though."

"You won't. If it doesn't work, we'll just go back to the way things were. It might be a little awkward at first, but it will be fine. We've talked about this at length, and Datch and I are both fine with it."

"Yes, we wouldn't have asked you if we weren't sure."

"So, what happens now?"

Carina turned and gave Krissy a long, slow kiss on the lips. Just as Peebop came walking in the door from the rest of the ship. He stopped, looked at them for a moment, and headed back out the door, stepping very quietly.

Datch then also gave Krissy a big kiss and then they all sat back and took another drink.

"That." Said Carina. "And we let the rest just happen."

"But not now." Added Datch. "We are sitting next to a war zone. It may be a little off putting."

They all laughed.

Just then the cargo bay door opened and Tate came walking in with Kato.

"Wow, you've kept the bar?" she said looking around.

Further in the ship, Peebop arrived back at the rec room.

"You won't believe what I just saw." he said.

"What?" said Fred looking up.

"Carina was giving Krissy a kiss in front of Datch."

"A quick peck on the cheek?"

"No, A full blown kiss on the lips."

"She was?"

"Yes."

"I told you something is going on." Said Dapo.

"What?" said Hagger.

"I spotted Datch and Carina kissing Krissy in the bar on the space station." Said Dapo.

Fred was thoughtful for a moment.

"Look, folks, if they want to have a three-way relationship, it's up to them. Don't go interfering. I'll have a quiet word with Datch and make sure everything is all right with Carina, okay?"

He looked around the room at the others.

"Okay?" he said again.

They all looked at him and nodded.

"Good. Right, let's find another film to watch."

Just then, Datch stuck his head through the door. They all turned and looked at him.

"Err, Kato and Tate have just come and told us that we are invited to dinner with the King," he said.

They were all looking at him. He checked to see if someone was standing behind him.

"What?" he said.

"Nothing," said Fred. "What time does he want us?"

"Err, 8pm. Posh dress code. OK?"

"That's about five hours then," added Tank.

"Yes. Five hours," repeated Datch.

"We're going to play one of the racing games if you guys want to come to the cargo bay."

"Thanks," said Fred.

He left them still looking at the doorway.

"Folks, you need to stop looking at them like that. One, it looks really creepy, and two, it will make them feel uncomfortable. If they're having a relationship, it's their own business. Okay?"

They all nodded again.

"I mean it!"

"Okay," said Rosey.

Dapo and Hagger decided to join in the racing game. Tish and Rosey decided to watch. Fred decided to go and keep an eye on Rosey and Tish.

In deep space, one of the damaged rebel ships limped into the base in the Garhar system. It was badly damaged, and the pilot had managed to save himself by jury-rigging the interspace drive. He was not in good shape, even with nanobots in his body. The radiation from the interspace drive had poisoned him, as he had to run it without the normal shielding, and the nanobots could not repair all the damage. He had a few weeks left to live at best, and he was having to take nanobots every few hours to keep going.

He was not going to die without taking revenge for all his friends who were now floating dead in space. He went over to a second ship and powered up the systems. Ten minutes later, he left the base, heading for the Klayton star system at interspace nineteen. There was a contact there who should be able to help him.

The next three hours passed by, and Datch, Carina, and Krissy were just being their normal selves, much to the annoyance of Rosey and Tish. They were both hoping to see something that would give them a reason to ask.

Finally, they headed off to their rooms to get changed.

Two hours later, two large limousines pulled up outside the back of the Raven.

The Pack walked down the ramp. The men were in suits, and the ladies were in evening dresses.

"Err, how do we talk to the King?" asked Krissy as they walked over to the back of the first limousine.

"Well, he's not our king, so I think 'Sir' should be okay. I'll ask him if he minds first, though," said Datch.

A man got out of the passenger seat and opened the door for them.

Datch, Krissy, and Carina got into the first limousine with Rosey, Tish, Dapo, and Hagger. Behind them, the rest of The Pack got into the second limousine. Shortly afterwards, the vehicles departed, heading for the palace.

There was a team of workmen repairing the wall where the plasma cannon had been destroyed, and gardeners were busy fixing all the damage done to the gardens.

The limousines pulled up, and two members of staff opened the doors for them. Datch got out, followed by the rest. A member of the staff then led the way through some large doors and into the palace.

They were shown into a very ornate room with many paintings of previous kings and queens hanging on the walls. It had a lot of ornate furniture with fancy gold edgings. A number of staff were also on hand, holding trays of drinks.

"Ladies and gentlemen, the King will be with you shortly," said a man in a very smart suit.

"Thank you," said Datch.

He picked up a glass of something that looked like sparkling wine from a tray that was being offered around by one of the staff.

Five minutes later, the commander came in, followed by Kato and Tate. They were all in dress uniforms with feathers and fancy collars.

"Hello everyone," said the commander as he came over.

"Hello, Commander," said Datch, taking a sip of his wine.

"Oh, just call me Paul," the commander said.

"OK, Paul it is," said Datch, smiling.

"So, what has happened to the rebels and the princess?" asked Hagger.

"At the moment, they are residing in a maximum-security facility while the King decides what to do with them."

"Don't the criminal services decide that?" asked Carina.

"No, they have committed treason against the crown and as such the King decides their fate."

"What about Dirk?"

"He left the star system three hours ago en route to the galactic centre."

"Hopefully, that's the last we'll ever see of him." added Kato.

Datch turned and looked at her.

"Well, it looks like you and Tate got your jobs back." he said.

"Not quite. We are both now assigned to the King's protective services."

"Oh, promotion. Cool." added Krissy.

"Err, yes. Sort of."

"So, what's next for you guys?" asked Tate.

"We have about six days before the next gig so we're heading to the beach resort we talked about for a bit of relaxation before starting work again."

"I can't wait to get under the palm trees." added Rosey.

"I'm looking forward to a nice cold beer without having to chase anyone." said Clax.

"Me too." added Tish.

Just then, two guards came in the door followed by a man dressed in a posh red and gold suit. He stopped in front of the doors and stepped to the left.

"Ladies and gentlemen, may I present King Winthrop the twelfth," he said in a very loud voice.

The King came walking through the doors. He stopped and waited. Paul, Kato, and Tate all bowed, and The Pack followed suit. Afterwards, the King came over to them.

"Kato, could you do the honours, please?" he asked.

"Certainly, your Majesty."

"This is Datch, your Majesty."

Datch gave a little bow, and the King held out his hand for Datch to shake.

"Pleased to meet you, your Majesty," he said, and shook the King's hand.

Kato introduced the King to each member of The Pack. When he had finished, he turned to face them all.

"Before we have dinner, I would just like to say thank you to all of you. You have most likely saved the monarchy. You have managed to defeat some very devious people and did not just stop and go on your way, leaving our world to what could have been a fate worse than death. I give you my word that if you ever need my help, I shall do my utmost to help you."

Datch stepped forward.

"Your Majesty, you are very welcome. Err, please excuse me if I'm a bit forward, but can we call you 'sir'? It's much easier to say."

The King laughed.

"Yes, I think 'sir' will be fine."

He turned and looked at the man near the door and gave a small nod.

"Now I think it is time to eat," he said.

They followed him into a dining room.

The dining room was very large, and it had a large table in the centre that ran almost the entire length of it. The table was laid out with fine silver cutlery and very fine porcelain plates, which had gold running around the edges. There were a number of staff standing waiting to help the guests to be seated. Everyone waited until the King sat down before sitting down themselves.

"I do apologise if my aide's research is a little lacking into your dining customs. I'm sure you will understand that he only had an hour to find out about the Bellatrixian culture." said the King.

"I'm sure everything will be great, sir," said Datch.

The King smiled and rang a little bell that was sitting next to him. The door opened, and a number of waiters came in carrying trays of food. They fanned out across the room, delivering the starters to the waiting guests.

The meal consisted of four courses. The first was a vegetable soup with freshly baked bread. This was followed with what looked like a roast boar accompanied with roast Kella and other assorted vegetables.

Then came the sweet.

The king cleared his throat,

"I'm terribly sorry but we have been unable to get chocolate ice cream that I understand you like so my aid has suggested this Quarcar fruit one instead."

"I'm sure it will be wonderful, sir." Said Carina.

They had the sweet, which was indeed wonderful, and Datch made a note to suggest it to the ice cream company at home. That was then followed by a selection of cheeses and crackers.

Afterwards, the King led the guests to another room for after-dinner drinks.

Datch was starting to think that he would explode if he ate anything more and was feeling twice the weight he normally did. He did a mental check to find out if the gravity was different to Bellatrix, only to find out it was slightly less. This made him feel even more full.

He stood talking to Kato and trying to get the food to digest a bit when the King came walking over.

"Did you enjoy the meal?" asked the King.

"Yes, sir. I enjoyed it very much. In fact, I'm feeling rather on the full side."

"Good, well I hope your trousers hold up." He said and laughed.

"I'm sure they will, sir. We normally have light meals due to working a lot of the time."

"Yes, I understand you have another concert soon?" he asked.

"Yes, sir, in just under a week on Klayton. We have two gigs there and then we're off to the Gack system."

"How long have you been performing together?"

"About nine Bellatrixian years, sir."

"So, that would be about fourteen of our years then?"

"I believe so, sir."

"I would come to see you perform, but from what my aid has told me it is not my type of music. I'm more a classical man myself. Maybe in a few years when my new heir is old enough, you could come back and do a performance in the city by royal commandment, of course."

"That would be very cool, sir."

Datch paused for a moment and looked thoughtful.

"Sir, may I ask what is going to happen to the Princess?"

The King looked thoughtful for a moment.

"Hmm. She is going to spend a while at a palace in the mountains under guard. In the meantime, I'm going to have a male heir or two so that she can never have the throne."

"I can't believe she fooled us the way she did, sir."

"My daughter has turned out to be a very devious person. Please don't let her behaviour put our planet in a bad light. We are normally a very polite and helpful people."

"No, sir. We won't. Kato and Tate are very honourable, and they have set a very good example. One bad apple does not mean the whole bunch is rotten."

The King's aid had looked up The Pack on the galactic database and had informed the king about his findings. The Pack had a lot of friends in some very important places. The wrong word from them, and the planet could find itself with a lot of questions being asked about it.

"Yes, Kato and Tate have both proved themselves very loyal. That's why they have been moved to my protection squad. With you being famous across the galaxy, how do you deal with security?"

"Oh, we have Timbo, sir."

The King looked across the room at Timbo, who was currently blocking the light from one of the windows.

"Yes, I see how that would work." Said the King smiling.

"Does the traveling bother you?"

"Not really, we like exploring, so it allows us to work and have fun at the same time. Do you travel much, sir?"

I have a lot of commitments, so yes. But I do try to keep it to a minimum."

They went on to talk about Bellatrix and Welly Four. Finally, at around midnight, The Pack were taken back to the Raven. The king had offered for them to stay in the palace, but Datch graciously declined. It had been a busy few weeks, and they wanted to leave early in the morning.


Next morning, The Pack all filed into the cockpit. Datch was already sitting in his seat and turned to the rest of them when they had all sat down.

"I think it's time for some rest and relaxation. We have seven days on the beach."

"Well, don't just sit there and talk about it. Let's get going," said Tank.

Datch turned to the front and put his headset on.

"Palace control, this is Raven ready to depart on route to Hybaysus."

"Raven, flight path will be clear in two minutes. Lock on to beacon 00017 and prepare for launch."

"Thanks, Control. Locking on."

Fifteen minutes later, they were leaving orbit for free space.

"Raven, set course for Hybaysus interspace seventeen."

"Course laid in. Do you wish standard alarm?"

"No. Alarm ten minutes before arrival, please. Engage interspace drive."

The stars outside winked out and started to flicker.

"Ten minutes?" said Clax.

"Hey, we're at interspace seventeen. It's a three-hour trip," said Datch.

"Good point. Just time for another couple of coffees then."

They headed to the rec room to have a coffee and watch a movie.

# Hybaysus six

Three hours later, they were on approach to Hybaysus Six. The star was a large white dwarf with twelve planets orbiting it. The first five were quite close to the star. Two of them were also a binary, orbiting each other as they orbited the star. The sixth one out was just at the right distance for a warm climate and almost Bellatrixian temperatures. It was also a short two-hour trip at interspace seventeen to Klayton for the next gig. This allowed them to stay there until the morning before the gig, when they needed to do their sound check.

The planet Hybaysus Six was more green than blue, and the water was not so much in oceans as in vast lakes that were dotted all over its surface and connected with large open rivers. This made the planet look like it was some sort of deranged dot-to-dot puzzle that had been drawn on a very large ball by someone with a very unsteady hand who was also using a large crayon. The planet Hybaysus Six was a terraformed world and had been created as a second planet for the Klayton star system, but only had a small population compared to the home world, with just five cities and various resorts and farms spread out around the planet. It was also a small world with only half the gravity of that on Bellatrix.

The Raven dropped down through the clouds, and below them was thousands of acres of thick tropical jungle. There were no roads or infrastructure across the surface, just a few tracks running into the trees from fruit processing plants. Most of the transportation was via the rivers or by air, leaving the jungle virtually untouched.

They flew down one of the rivers, passing over boats and cargo ships before the river opened out into a large sparkling lake. Datch started to slow down as they approached the resort. It was on the shores of the lake, with forests of tropical trees running down to the shoreline. The trees seemed to be a cross between a pine tree and a palm, with large leaves that gave lots of shade.

Datch brought the Raven in for a landing at one of the villas' landing pads. A number of porters were on hand to escort everyone to their villas.

They had booked six of them, as the villas were only three bedrooms, and had made sure they were all next to each other. Each one had its own splash pool, jacuzzi, sauna, and beachfront area. The complex also had a number of pools, three restaurants, and five bars. There was also a large outdoor amphitheatre which had bands and singers on in the evenings. Behind the resort complex was a small village with shops and a couple of restaurants, which were all nestled in the jungle and made to look almost invisible to the resort.

The Pack settled down on the beach, apart from the girls and Tank, who had all headed off in a limo to the local village for a bit of shopping. Rosey had said they needed a bit of "chilled retail therapy" to unwind after the last couple of weeks.

Hagger and Dapo decided to go and do a bit of snorkelling. Clax and Peebop were trying to fish off a small wooden jetty just down from Datch and Fred. They appeared to be doing a very good job of catching a lot of invisible fish, much to Datch and Fred's amusement.

Fred took the opportunity to talk to Datch.

"Datch, we've all noticed that you're getting very close to Krissy. Is everything okay with you and Carina?"

Datch smiled. It was bound to be picked up sooner or later.

"Yes, we're good. We're both sort of having a polyamorous relationship with Krissy, just to see if it will work."

"Tell me to shut up if I'm prying, but we wanted to make sure things were okay."

Datch laughed.

"No, you're good, Fred."

"How does Carina feel about it?"

"It was her idea."

"It was?"

"Yes, she got me to ask Krissy."

"And you were okay with that?"

"Yes, I like her too. So, it just made sense to give it a try."

"And Krissy?"

"Well, I think it blew her mind at first, but she said she wants to give it a try."

"Oh, okay. As long as it's all good. We spend a lot of time together, and I was worried about any friction, that was all."

"Fred, you can ask me anything. I've learned a lot from you, and I value everything you say."

"Thank you."

"Okay, now watch this."

Datch got up and took a spare pair of trunks out of a bag along with his snorkelling set. He walked up the beach a little way past the little jetty so that Clax and Peebop had their backs towards them and then covertly entered the water.

Fred watched as the top of Datch's snorkel moved closer to the little jetty and then disappeared underneath it.

A few moments later, Clax's line started to twitch. "Hey, I've got one." He said and started pulling at the line.

A moment later Peebop's line started twitching as well.

"I've got one to." he said.

"I must have a big one. It's really fighting me."

"Mine too."

A few moments later, they both pulled really hard, and a pair of trunks shot out of the water. They both fell backwards on the jetty, and the trunks did a double flip in the air before landing on top of Peebop's head.

Fred was laughing at them, and to make matters worse, Datch surfaced and looked at them.

"Guys! Can I have my trunks back please?"

Clax looked at Datch, then at Fred, and then back at Peebop, who was holding the trunks.

"Err, yes," said Peebop, and threw them at Datch.

Datch caught them and then came walking out of the water, wearing his other trunks. At that point, it dawned on Clax and Peebop that they had just been had. They looked at each other, got up, and ran after Datch. They grabbed him and threw him back in the water.

At that point, Fred fell off his sunbed because he was laughing so hard. Clax and Peebop then grabbed Fred and threw him in the water. Datch grabbed Clax and pulled him in, followed by Peebop. The four of them had five minutes of splashing about before they returned to their sunbeds, laughing.

"So, what's the plan for tonight?" said Clax getting his breath back.

"Party time, I think. There is a good band on tonight in the amphitheatre and they are our style of music."

"Cool."

The girls came back, and they also thought the amphitheatre sounded like a great idea.

That evening, they headed over to one of the restaurants and had a very good steak dinner before going to the amphitheatre.

The amphitheatre had been carved out of the bedrock and had seating around the edge that went up several tiers. The centre was a large, flat oval, and a stage had been constructed at one end. It had two large speaker stacks on either side of the stage and a lighting rig above it.

The Pack decided that front-row seats were a good idea, as they were planning to have a dance. The resort had the foresight to place a second lighting rig above the open area in front of the stage, creating a large dance floor. They had also put on an outdoor bar at the opposite end for the guests.

They collected their drinks and sat down. The amphitheatre soon filled up, and then it was time for the band to take the stage. The music was a mix of rock and pop that made you want to dance.

It didn't take long before The Pack were up dancing, and then the band started playing "Supernova". Well, The Pack couldn't help themselves and started singing along with it. Moments later, Datch's and Carina's rings energised and turned into columns of light, which then spread to the others, including Krissy. It was the first time they had noticed her energise at the same time, as normally she would be half a song behind.

Other guests stood back as The Pack danced around the floor, and then guest followed guest as the energy spread across the dance floor, making them sparkle as it went. Then it reached the band on the stage, and they started sparkling. They were looking at themselves as they played, and then the music took hold of them, and they played the best set they had ever done. Afterwards, a DJ came on, looked at the crowd, shrugged his shoulders, and went into his booth.

The evening went very well, and The Pack didn't need lights to see their way back to the villas. Krissy was staying in Datch and Carina's, and they were making the most of it. It was taking some getting used to, but Datch and Carina were true to their word and took things very slowly with her.


Above them, a ship came into orbit. Its scanning array looked down at the surface, searching the world below. It found its target. The pilot took the ship down to the surface, landing in a clearing in the jungle a few kilometers from the target. He shut down the systems and headed out of the ship, picking up a bag on the way that had several weapons in it and a large cylindrical device.


The next morning, Datch woke up only to find himself sandwiched between Krissy and Carina. He needed to use the bathroom and lay there, pondering how to get there without waking either of them up. Finally, he decided that the best way was to crawl down the bed and out of the bottom. It took him a few moments, but eventually he dropped onto the floor at the bottom of the bed. He breathed a sigh of relief and headed to the bathroom. The whole three-way relationship was going to take a bit more thinking about. It was great all sleeping together, but the getting up for the bathroom was another thing. After he had relieved himself, he decided to go and lie on the couch and leave the girls to sleep.

An hour and a half later, someone called his name, and he opened his eyes. Carina was standing in front of him with a coffee.

"Morning, babes," he said.

"Morning. Are you okay?"

"Yes, why?"

"You're out here."

"Oh, well, I needed the bathroom and then didn't want to disturb you, so I came here."

"Thank you. That was very thoughtful."

"Is Krissy awake?"

"Yes, I am," came a voice from the kitchen.

"Morning," said Datch.

"Morning. I'm making Jeader rolls. Do you want some?" came the voice from the kitchen.

"Yes, please. Can I have two?"

"Sure, coming right up."

Datch took a drink of the coffee.

"So, what are we doing today?" asked Datch.

"We were talking about going to the beach, and maybe me and Krissy are going to head to the shops. I think I'm going to get something for my mum. I spotted a figurine she would like. Also, Krissy wants to get something for your mum."

"Okay, the beach it is then."

Krissy came in with the breakfast, and they all sat down eating it.

"Krissy, I hope last night was okay for you, and we didn't go too fast?" asked Datch.

"Yes, it was great, thanks. I had a lot of fun."

"Good," said Carina.

"I'm just wondering if there is a better way of sleeping though," said Datch.

"Why?" asked Krissy.

"Well, it was a bit of a squeeze getting out to go for a pee."

"Oh, if you like, I can sleep in the middle next time," said Krissy.

"Hmm, yes, but what if you need to go?" said Datch.

"I see your point."

They sat eating their Jeader rolls and thinking about the problem.

"Maybe if the ones who have drunk the most sleep on the outside, then that way the person in the middle will be less likely to want to go."

"Yes, but what if they do?"

"I know, why don't we just swap positions?" said Carina.

"How?"

"Well, if say you're in the middle and need to go, then wake one of us enough to get past, and then they roll over into your spot."

"It might work. I wouldn't mind, and I'd just go back to sleep again." said Krissy.

"Okay, that sounds like a plan," said Datch.

"Yes, let's try it next time." Added Carina.

They finish their breakfast and then after Datch had got dressed they headed to the beach.

In the jungle, a door on an old shack opened, and a man came out. He was quite tall and muscular, with brown and grey hair and dark brown eyes. He had a yellowish-grey complexion and had a number of blisters on his skin that were weeping small amounts of blood. He was wearing combat clothes and carried a small backpack on his back. He stopped and coughed up some blood. I don't have long, he thought to himself.

He made his way through the jungle to the back of the resort and then worked his way along the perimeter fence until he found a road heading to the little village. He stopped and looked around before finding himself a place to sit where he was hidden but could still see the comings and goings of people. He needed to find a way in. He took another nanobot pill. It was every two hours now, and according to the medical scanner, he had about two or three days left. In the last twelve hours of that, he would not be able to move much as his muscles would have deteriorated too far. He set his military scanner to wake him if anyone came by and settled down for a rest. With this much radiation in his body, every movement was a mini-marathon.

On the beach, The Pack were making the most of their time off. Most of them were lying on sunbeds, and a waiter was sorting out their lunch. The lunch consisted of various containers with fries and Hacks wings, which also had various pots of sauce to accompany them.

They sat on the sunbeds eating lunch.

"Krissy, are we going shopping after lunch?" asked Carina.

"Yes, I can do," said Krissy.

"Anyone else want to come?"

"We went before we came to the beach. I think you were all asleep," said Rosey.

"Oh, okay, we must have been. Looks like just me and you, then," said Krissy.

They finished their food, and afterwards, Krissy and Carina headed off to the shops.

# Revenge

Carina and Krissy arrived at the gatehouse. Through the gate was a little road that led down to the village. The security guard on the gate opened it for them, and they headed through it and started walking down the lane.

"So, what's the plan?" asked Krissy.

"Let's go to the shop where we spotted all the souvenirs yesterday and then call in at the café on the way back."

"Sounds good."

The lane had tall trees down either side, giving respite from the sun's heat. Krissy and Carina walked near the edge of the road to make the most of the shade.

Hidden in the undergrowth, a small scanner started to beep. The rebel opened his eyes and looked at the scanner. It was detecting a Bellatrixian. He looked out through the bushes and spotted Carina and Krissy walking down the road. He looked at the scanner again. It couldn't identify the other lifeform, which was odd, but the red-headed female was definitely Bellatrixian. His contact had said that the people who caused the death of his friends were Bellatrixian.

He watched as they walked by, heading down the road, and got his gun ready to fire. He stopped himself. This wasn't the plan. Anyway, if it wasn't them, he would give himself away. He had other plans for the red head. He realized that he was contradicting himself in his mind. Must be the radiation, he thought.

He decided to get closer to them and maybe if he got within earshot, they would give themselves away. He waited until they were a good distance down the road before casually walking out of the undergrowth and following them into the village.

The village was laid out in circles, with roads dividing the buildings into rings. The road from the resort led through the rings to the centre, where there were a number of shops, restaurants, recreational facilities, and cafés.

Carina looked at Krissy as they approached the centre. "Krissy, I know this sounds silly, but it feels like someone's watching us."

"Hmm, yes. I feel it too."

They stopped and started to look around. The rebel noticed them stop and turned down a side street. They looked behind them up the street. No one was following them, just a few people going about their business. An old man walking his dog. The dog was barking at something down a side street. There was a couple of women chatting to each other as they walked along.

They couldn't see anything that looked out of place.

They turned back towards the centre and started heading down the road.

The rebel stopped for another nanobot infusion and then added an adrenaline boost. He winced with pain as the new nanobots tried to repair his failing body. He headed down another street that led to the centre and came out into the central plaza.

The central plaza was quite busy, with a lot of people shopping and relaxing. A delivery of fresh fruit was being delivered to one of the shops by a drone, and there was a queue outside of the butcher's. He casually looked around and spotted Krissy and Carina going into one of the souvenir shops. After a moment's thought, he decided to go and sit down on a seat that was in the shade. The sun was far too hot for him, as his body was burning up with the radiation.

He was starting to have trouble remembering things as the radiation was spreading through his brain. Another fifty-six hours and he would be dead. Even if he was transferred to a new body, the damage was too great to repair it. No, this was it, and he wasn't going to die alone.

Krissy and Carina stood looking at the souvenirs. There was quite a lot to choose from. Carina had already picked up the one that she had wanted for her mum, and now it was Krissy's turn to find something. There were a lot of small figures dressed in the local clothes and various pictures of the planet. There were also various placemats of views of the cities and lakes. Finally, Krissy decided on a towel with pictures of the lakes on.

They headed outside and crossed over the plaza to one of the cafés and sat down in the sun. The rebel watched them go and checked the pistol in his pocket. He thought for a moment and decided to wait until they were walking back. If he tried it here, he might fail. He needed to get them away from other people so he could take the red-headed female. That way he could get the others to come looking for her, and then he could take them all out.

Krissy and Carina finished their drinks and started to head back towards the holiday resort. The street was quiet, with just the occasional person walking down it from the resort. Behind them, the rebel walked alone, trying not to be noticed. He now had developed a limp, as one of his leg muscles was starting to deteriorate and was not working properly.

Krissy stopped to look at a bush with some strange-looking flowers on it.

"This looks nice," she said, admiring the bush.

"Yes, it does look nice," added Carina.

The rebel came up behind them.

"You two turn around very slowly!" he said.

They turned around and the rebel stood pointing a plasma pistol at them.

"What do you want?" asked Carina, looking at the gun.

"You. You're coming with me, and you," he said, pointing the pistol at Krissy, "tell her friends that they are to come alone or she dies."

Krissy was frozen to the spot, staring at the weapon.

"Move it!" he said, waving the gun at her.

"Go!" said Carina.

Krissy turned and ran up the road towards the resort. The rebel pointed to a small track leading off into the jungle.

"That way," he said.


Carina hesitated, but then she started to walk towards the track. The rebel followed her, keeping the gun trained on her back.

"That way!" he said.

"Who are you?" she asked as she started walking towards the small track.

"You and your friends caused the death of all my friends."

"You're one of the rebels?"

"I am the last of the rebels, as you put it, and it's payback time. Now move it."

Carina started to move down the track.

'Datch! Help me!' she thought.

On the beach, Datch was lying on his sunbed and suddenly sat up.

'Are you okay, babes?' he thought back to her.

'No, one of the rebels is here and has got me at gunpoint. He's leading me through the jungle. He says he wants payback.'

'Crap! Okay, we're coming just make a note of where you are going so that we can follow. Is Krissy okay?'

'Yes. She's running back to get you. He wants you to come after him alone.'

'Okay. Don't worry, I'm on my way.'

He jumped up out of the sunbed.

"Folks, Carina is in trouble, and we need to get to her!" he shouted.

"What?" said Fred, looking at him.

"One of the rebels has got her at gunpoint."

"Are you joking?" asked Clax.

Just at that point, Krissy came running down the beach shouting, "Datch!"

"Oh crap!" said Fred.

"Datch, Datch. Carina has been," she reached him.

"We know. Calm down." Said Datch.

"But. He's got a gun."

"Look, Carina is talking to me. It's one of the rebels after payback. We'll deal with him."

"What's up?" asked Rosey and Tish, running up the beach after hearing the shouting.

"One of the rebels has kidnapped Carina."

"Okay. You folks stay here. Clax, Fred, Peebop, you come with me."

"Datch, what are you doing?"

"Saving Carina!"

"Do you want me to come?" asked Timbo.

"Err. okay."

"Datch, we need to call in the security services."

"Yes, but it will take them a while to get here, and he may have killed her by then."

"Okay. But we're going to need to be careful."

"Okay, Hmm. Timbo, how do you feel about being shot at?"

"I don't think I want to do that."

"You would have a lot of shielding on. So, it won't hurt you."

"OK, if it will save Carina."

"Tank, you contact the security services and tell them what has happened. The rest of you look after Krissy. Right, let's go to the Raven."

Datch got up and started to head up the beach towards the villa followed by Fred, Clax, Peebop and Timbo while Tank headed to the security office.

Datch bounded up the ramp, through the cargo bay and straight into their room. By the time the others walked in he was walking back into the cargo bay with the two plasma rifles and their pistols.

"Clax, here, you take Carina's rifle, Peebop, Fred, takes these." He handed Clax the rifle and Fred and Peebop a pistol each."

"You're really going to take him out, aren't you?"

"He's got Carina and therefore he deserves it."

They looked at each other.

"Timbo, put this on and set it to maximum."

Datch handed him a personal shield generator.

Timbo put the shield on and powered it up. Datch put his on and did the same.

"OK, Fred shoot me."

"What!"

"Shoot me!"

Fred pointed the pistol at Datch and fired. He was knocked onto the floor by the round but got back up checking everything was still working.

"Well, that worked. Still, I think my ass is going to hurt a bit if I get knock down too many times."

"Do you want to shoot me too?" asked Timbo.

"Do you want me to?"

"Yes please."

Fred did and Timbo just stood there and grinned.

"Well, if we need a tank, we have one." Said Peebop.

“Timbo, put this on as well.”

Datch handed him the portable scattering field generator and then looked across the room at a large box with grey camouflage patterns on it.

“Timbo, I take it that box has another missile system in it?”

“Err, yes Datch.”

“Would you mind bringing it?”

“Sure Datch.”

“Err, Timbo. Don’t fire it at a building if Carina is in it, please.”

“OK.”

“Right let’s go.”

They came out of the back of the Raven and headed for the main gate.

When they arrived, Tank was standing outside. There was a noise inside the office, and a security officer came running out. He stopped and looked at them.

Datch and Clax were holding their rifles across their chests, ready to shoot anything they didn't like. Fred and Peebop had their pistols in holsters around their waists, like a pair of gunfighters, and Timbo had his missile system casually leaning against his shoulder. They had also put on combat clothes for effect.

"I was about to tell you to wait for the security services, but now I'm more worried about the jungle," said the guard.

"When they get here, just tell them to look for the smoke," said Datch.

The guard started to smile, thinking it was a joke, but then realized it wasn't.

"Oh," he said.

"Tank, here's a ship comms unit," said Datch, throwing a small device to him. "Only use it if necessary. I've got mine on silent, so just message me, and if I can, I'll open a comms channel, OK?"

"OK."

Datch looked into space for a while.

'Babes, you OK?'

There was a pause, and then Carina's voice popped into Datch's head.

'Yes, just about. He hasn't harmed me yet, and he's just making me follow the track.'

'Good. Where does the track start?'

'There's a bush about halfway to the village with purple leaves and bright orange and yellow flowers. The track is almost opposite and goes between two big trees.'

'OK, we're on our way. If he does anything else, let me know.'

'I'm very scared.'

'I know, we're coming. Just hang in there.'

Datch turned to the others.

"Come on, I know where he's taking her."

"Err, how?" said Peebop.

"They were singing together last night," said Fred.

"Oh yeah."

They walked down the road until they found the bush
Carina had told them about and stopped to look around.

"Over there," said Datch, pointing.

They walked across the road to an opening in the jungle.
Datch got out a small scanner and pressed a couple of
buttons.

The scanner beeped, then after a short pause, beeped
again. He looked closely at the screen and pressed a couple
more buttons, and it bleeped again.

'Carina, does he look unwell?'

In the jungle, Carina turned to look at the rebel. Now she
looked at him, she could see his eyes were bloodshot and his
skin looked grey. There were also traces of blood coming
from his eyes, ears, and nose.

"Are you okay?" she said.

"Shut up and move it!" he said, then coughed.

'Yes, very. He doesn't have much colour and it looks like
he's been bleeding. Why?'

'Don't let him get too close to you if you can. If this
scanner is right, he has extreme radiation poisoning and is
dying. The traces of blood it just picked up are radioactive.'

'Oh. Okay. I'll try.'

"You okay, Datch?" said Fred.

"Yes, I was just talking to Carina. The rebel has extreme
radiation poisoning. He's dying, so he's not going to be
bothered about killing himself at the same time as us."

"Oh, do you think he's going to use Carina to bait a trap?"

"Possibly, but I think he'll want to get as many of us at the same time. Also, if this scanner is right, he's taking nanobots to try and stay alive, and it looks like they're fighting a losing battle."

"If that's so, we can use that to our advantage." said Fred.

"How?"

"He's going to want us grouped up before he kills us. Also, Timbo and anyone standing next to him will be invisible if he's using a scanner."

"Hmm. Okay. Let's spread out a bit."

Further in the jungle, Carina was making sure her captor was staying as far away as possible without giving him any reason to get closer.

"Stop!" he said and walked past her to the foot of a tree.

He brushed a couple of leaves away and there was a small device hidden underneath. He pressed a little device in his pocket and the device started flashing a green light.

"Okay, move it!"

Carina moved past the device, looking for something to tell Datch where it was. She noticed a small bush with green and white flowers to the left of the trees where the device was.

He covered the device back up with leaves and when they had passed it, he turned and pressed the little device again. The device gave three little beeps.

"What's that?" she asked.

"It's a little present for your friends when they come looking for you. Now move it!"

She started moving along the path again.

'Datch, there's a mine on the path between two trees. There's a bush with green and white flowers on the left of it.'

'How big is the bush?'

'About the size of the kebab machine at home.'

'Okay. We'll look out for it. Thanks.'

"Guys, he's mined the path. Carina has told me to look for a bush with green and white flowers to the left of the path near two trees."

"Okay, let's be careful from here on in."

Meanwhile back at the resort, Tish and Rosey had calmed Krissy down.

"I don't understand why he didn't take me?" she said.

"I don't know. Maybe he wasn't sure who you are and thought you were a maid or something."

"Wait, I bet I know why." Said Hagger triumphantly.

"What?"

"She's from Sol, not Bellatrix. I bet he was looking for Bellatrixians."

"Hmmm, I wonder how he found out we were here?" Asked Dapo.

"I don't know. I'm going to the Raven to message Kato."

"Why the Raven?" asked Rosey.

"Err, I don't have her vid id."

"Oh. I do." She gave him a smug smile.

"Okay, you ask her then."

"I will."

She fetched out her vid com and sent Kato a message telling her what was going on. When she had done, she turned back to the others.

"There, done." she said.

"What did she say?" Asked Dapo.

"Give it chance. She's 40lys away. My vid com said it was going to take seven minutes to get there."

"Oh."

"So, what now?" asked Hagger.

"You're going to get Krissy a strong drink." Said Rosey looking at him with the expression of someone on a mission.

He obediently got up and went to fetch it.

"How do you do that? If I tell Dapo to do things like that, he just looks at me." Said Tish.

"It took a lot of work but if he does as he's told he gets rewarded later."

"OK, no more details needed."


In the jungle, Carina spotted a small shack in the undergrowth.

"Stop!" said the rebel.

He pressed the little device in his pocket. A number of little beeps were heard. Carina looked around, trying to work out where the mines were.

"Move to the door!" he motioned to the shack.

'Datch, I'm at some shack in the jungle. There are a number of mines about fifty metres from it, and they're spread out. I tried to work out where they are, but they all beeped at once.'

'Don't worry, we've got it covered. Just try to stay as safe as you can, and we'll get to you.'

The rebel opened the door and pushed Carina inside.

Inside was an old-looking table with a bag sitting on top of it. There were two old wooden chairs, one of which was sitting in the centre of a metal ring that was on the floor.

"Sit down over there," he said, pointing to it.

Carina went over and sat down. He reached into the bag on the table and fetched out another control box. He pressed one of the buttons, and an energy field shot up around Carina.

"Just in case you get any ideas," he said, and fetched out a packet of nanobots. He took four out of the packet and swallowed them.

"What are you going to do with me?" Carina asked.

"You're my bait for your friends. When they get here, I'll kill them and then you."

"They will have called the security services."

"I don't care. By the time they get here, I'll be dead. I have radiation poisoning and only have a few hours at best. There's a thermonuclear device in this bag, and when I die, it will detonate, taking out everything for ten kilometres."

"Why kill everyone else?"

"Why not?" he laughed. "Now shut up and make peace with your gods."

'Datch, he's dying and he has a bomb in here that will detonate when he dies. He says it will level the whole area, including the village and the resort.'

Datch stopped and thought for a moment.

'In which case, we'll have to destroy it before it goes off.'

'What?'

'Timbo has his toys with him.'

'I'm in here.'

'I know, don't worry.'

Carina started to worry a lot.

Datch fetched out the communicator and pressed it.

"Tank, you there?"

"Yes, Datch. How's it going?"

"Err, we have a bit of an issue."

"Issue?"

"Yes, the rebel has a big bomb that if it goes off, it will level the resort and the village."

"What!"

"Yes, and the really bad news is that the bomb is linked to the rebel's health and if he dies, it goes off."

"Oh crap! Are you coming back?"

"Hell no! Tell the others to get into the Raven and put its shields up. Also, notify the security services."

"OK, Datch."

Tank went running into the office and told the security guard before running back to the others.

Fred turned to Datch.

"Datch, what are you planning to do? Our personnel shields won't stand that sort of blast. We'll die."

"I don't intend to. I have a plan."

They all gathered around and Datch explained what he was planning to do. Afterwards, they all stepped back.

"You're mad, you know that?" said Clax.

"Yes, I know."

"Well, I like my bit." Said Timbo.

"You would." Said Fred.

They carried on up the track towards the shack. They reached the place where Carina had said the first mine was.

'Carina, there will be an explosion and screaming outside. Look frightened. It is just an act though, okay?'

'Okay.'

"Timbo, you ready for this?"

"Yes, Datch."

"Is your shield at full power?"

"Yes, Datch."

"Okay, go for it."

Timbo went walking over to the mine. What happened next was a very loud explosion and blast of light as the mine detonated, blowing a very big hole in the ground. Also, Datch and Peebop screamed Fred's name out loudly and one of the two trees fell over. Timbo, however, did not fall over. Instead, he just turned around and grinned.

In the shack, the rebel turned to Carina.

"Looks like at least one of your friends has taken their last breath." He said and laughed.

"You monster!" yelled Carina and banged on the shield. Sparkles of energy shone brightly as she hit it.

'We're all good by the way.' Came a voice in her head.

'Okay.'

She carried on banging the shield for a bit before sitting down and pretending to cry.

Back at the resort, they heard an explosion. Tank was sitting in Clax's seat. He hit the comms button.

"Guys!"

"Yes?"

"You guys alright?"

"Yes, that was Timbo removing a tree."

"Oh."

"There may be a few more loud bangs soon. Don't worry about them."

"What's he doing, removing the forest so he can see him better?"

"Err, not at the moment but we'll think about it."

Tank looked at the control panel and could swear it was grinning at him.

"What was that?" Said Rosey running into cockpit.

Tank turned to her with a look of disbelief on his face.

"Err, I think that was Datch and Timbo having fun."

"Having fun!"

"Yes. Timbo is apparently removing some of the jungle."

He turned back to the control panel to see if it was still grinning. It wasn't.

Back in the jungle, Datch spotted the shack. It was in amongst some trees in a less dense part of the jungle and was free of undergrowth, allowing anyone inside to see around the building. The shack itself was made of metal with a wooden door.

'Carina, we can see the shack. Where is he?'

Carina looked up.

'He's sitting in a chair by the door holding a gun and his control device.'

'OK, look at the door carefully and tell me what you see.'

'It looks like it is made of wood and has five panels across with a piece of wood across the bottom, middle, and top. The middle one has the lock on it.'

'Good, now where is he in relation to the lock?'

'He is a little way from it.'

'OK, there is going to be another explosion in a minute, maybe two. If he moves anywhere near the lock with the controller, tell me.'

'OK.'

Outside, Timbo put down his missile launcher and walked towards the minefield. Datch and Clax lay down on the ground and took aim on the door. Fred and Peebop went over to the far side and got ready to fire.

Datch nodded at Timbo, and he walked casually up the path like he was out for an afternoon stroll. There was a large explosion that shook the shack. Carina could see Timbo out of the dirty window. His shield lit up like a supernova as the energy was reflected away from it. The rebel jumped out of his chair and carefully looked out of the window. Timbo was grinning.

"Holy crap! What is that?" he said.

A number of plasma bolts came flying through the window. The rebel ducked back behind the door.

'Second panel in next to the lock,' Carina thought.

Datch fired twice, and two plasma bolts came flying through the door, hitting the rebel's arm that was holding the controller. The bolts took the rebel's hand off, knocking his hand and the controller to the floor.

He went to try and grab it, but another volley of shots came through what was left of the window. He stepped back to the corner of the room out of the way of the shots and tried to work out what to do.

'He's in the corner behind the door,' thought Carina.

Datch looked at Timbo and waved his arms, pointing at the corner of the shack. Timbo nodded and started to walk to the shack. There was another explosion, and Carina looked at the rebel in the eyes.

"I think you may have upset Timbo!" she said in a very calm voice.

He looked at her. She was not afraid of him anymore, which scared him.

The walls of the shack then started folding in around him, pinning him in amongst the twisted metal and wood. He tried to move, but something was stopping him.

'Is he secure?' came a voice in Carina's head.

'Yes, Timbo has him trapped.'

From where she was standing, she could see two very large arms wrapping around the metal that was imprisoning the rebel.

Datch kicked what was left of the door down and walked in. Carina was still trapped behind the forcefield. He looked at the severed hand on the floor still holding the controller and picked it up.

The rebel looked at him.

"You will all die. As soon as my heart stops, boom! You're all dead!"

Datch prized the controller out of the severed hand and, after looking at it for a moment, turned to the rebel.

"I wouldn't count on it," he said and pressed a button.

The shield around Carina disappeared. She came over to him and gave him a hug.

"Shall we go?" she said.

"You had better run. That hit made the nanobots stop their current operation, and I'm starting to die. I win!"

Datch turned to him and grinned. "NO, you have lost, you just don't realise it!"

He turned and walked calmly out of the shack with Carina.

Timbo dropped the twisted metal with the rebel inside to the floor and followed Datch back to the missile launcher.

"Err, what about the bomb?"

"It can't explode if it doesn't exist." Said Fred, walking up.

"You're going to blow up the bomb!"

"Not quite. Timbo, if you would do the honours."

"Yes, Datch."

Timbo picked up the missile launcher and aimed it at the shack.

Carina watched in disbelief as Timbo fired a missile at the shack, hitting the metal remains and stopping next to the table with the bomb on it.

"OK, hit the deck!" said Datch.

Timbo hit the destruct button and the quantum drive inside the missile went into overload. The lines of force used to propel the missile in interspace started to collapse in on themselves. At this point, the nuclear bomb tried to detonate. Unfortunately for the detonator, the atoms in the bomb were now having a lot of trouble trying to stay in one piece, let alone trying to get friendly at a subatomic level. All the high-energy particles stopped feeling energetic and went to sleep. Finally, the atoms were overwhelmed by the collapsing interspace field. A nanosecond later, the shack, bomb, and the rebel vanished with a loud pop and a bright flash of light.

Due to the interspace field and its interaction with normal space, the entire collection of atoms reappeared in the local star's photosphere, where they were promptly ripped apart.

Carina looked at the smoking hole where the shack had been.

"What just happened?"

"Err, they went pop." Said Datch.

"Well, I know that."

"The Interspace drive caused a small but very intense gravity well as the drive self-destructed. The matter will have been ejected to the nearest stable gravity well."

Carina was quiet for a moment.

"You mean it ended up in the star?"

"Err, yes."

"And if we had been too close?"

"We would have too. We did read the instructions first." Datch said.

"And what did they say?"

"Do not use indoors. Do not shoot at people, and do not be within fifty meters of any detonation."

"Anything else?"

"Yes. Keep out of reach of children."

She looked at them and then back at the smoking hole.

"Can I suggest a beer is in order?" said Fred, changing the subject before Carina asked to see the rest of the instructions and they all got into trouble.

"Sounds like a plan." Added Clax.

They dusted themselves down and started to walk back through the jungle to the resort.

Clax had a quick look over his shoulder to check they hadn't accidentally opened an interspatial rift that didn't want to close and that it wasn't about to suck the entire contents of the planet into its star.

Other than the small wisps of smoke slowly raising from the hole it all looked good.

They found their way back to the road just as a detachment of security officers with some very large guns came running down the road towards them. They stopped in front of them, and the lead officer looked them up and down. Datch's party looked like some misfit raiding group that had been out for an afternoon stroll.

"Folks, there is a mad man on the loose. You need to get back to the resort."

Datch looked at him for a moment. He looked like quite a young officer and had a worried look on his face.

"Don't worry, officer. He's not on the loose anymore. It might be an idea to fence off the smoking hole in the jungle for a bit. It may be a little bit radioactive."

"What hole?"

"Well, your mad man kidnapped my wife. We didn't like that."

The officer looked puzzled.

"What about the hole?"

"It was where he was standing with a nuclear bomb."

"And that caused the hole?"

"No, our interspace missile caused the hole when we caused all the atoms in the bomb and the rebel to cease to exist along with the surrounding area."

The officer put his head on one side for a moment.

"We will need a memory download of the events, sir." he said.

"Sure, but can we have a beer first?"

The officer looked at the six of them and decided that the download could wait while they went to check on the hole.

"OK, sir. But please do not leave the planet."

"We don't intend to until the weekend, sir."

"Now where is this hole?"

"Follow that track over there and keep a lookout near the hole as there may be a mine or two that we missed."

"Thank you, sir. We will."

The group of officers headed off into the jungle while Datch and friends headed back to the resort.


They ambled up the road looking like they had just come from a war zone. Timbo was casually carrying the missile launcher in his arms with the launch tubes leaning against his shoulder, whereas Datch and Clax had slung their rifles over their shoulders. Datch was holding hands with Carina, and they were all relaxed. They approached the main gates, and the security guard they had seen earlier came running out.

"You folks okay?"

"Yes, you can tell everyone that it's all over now." said Fred.

"Are you sure?"

"Yes."

Datch walked up the ramp with Carina, followed by Peebop, Fred, Clax, and Timbo. The others came running into the cargo bay.

"Are you guys okay?" asked Rosey.

"Yes, we're fine," said Fred. "But we do need a drink."

"What happened to the rebel?" asked Tank.

"He, er, went pop," said Datch.

"Pop?" asked Rosey.

"Yes, pop. We'll tell you what happened while we have a drink. Carina, check yourself out with the medical scanner. You were close to him for quite a while."

"Okay," she said, and headed off with the other girls in tow.

There was a bang in the corner of the loading bay as Timbo put down the missile system. Datch took the rifle from Clax, and Fred and Peebop handed him their pistols. He headed into his and Carina's room and put them away. Carina was there with the girls. Rosey was moving the handheld medical scanner up and down her.

It beeped every now and again as it scanned her and then gave three short beeps. Rosey looked at it.

"It says you've been exposed to radiation and have received a mild dose," she said.

She looked closer at the readout.

"It also says it shouldn't harm you, but is recommending a small pack of nanobots just to be on the safe side."

"Raven, supply a pack of nanobots as per the medical scanner instructions," said Carina.

"The nanobots will be available in the recreation room shortly."

"I'll get them," said Krissy, leaving the room.

Datch walked over to Carina and gave her a very big hug. She looked at him for a moment.

"You were really worried, weren't you?" she said.

"Yes."

Rosey and Tish decided to go and leave Carina and Datch to it.

"I thought I had lost you," he said.

"I was scared, but not worried. I knew you were coming for me. I was sure it would be okay."

They kissed just as Krissy came walking through the door. She looked at them for a moment.

"Here, hurry up and take these. I don't want you both ill."

"Come here," said Carina, holding out her arm.

Krissy came over and they had a group hug.

Afterwards, Carina took her nanobots and they headed back to the others.

They had just arrived in the cargo bay when there was a roar of engines from outside. They headed outside just in time to see one of the Thoth spacecrafts touching down next to the Raven.

Datch, Carina, and Krissy walked down the Raven's ramp, followed by the others.

The ship's engines shut down, and the side door opened.

Kato, along with three other officers, came walking down the ramp.

"Hi, Kato," said Datch.

"Hi, Datch, Carina, folks. We heard you were having a spot of bother with one of the rebels, and the King told me to come straight away."

"We did. He kidnapped Carina."

"Err, I take it by the fact Carina is here, the matter has been resolved."

"Yes, he went pop," said Carina.

"Pop?"

"Yes, pop," said Datch. "We've just got back from the pop incident, and we're heading over to the bar for a beer to calm our nerves a bit. Come with us, and we'll explain what happened."

"Okay, sounds good."

Kato turned to the other officers.

"You two head back to the ship. The commander and I will join these people and find out what happened."

"Yes, sir."

Two of the men left and headed to the Thoth ship.

The Pack plus two headed over to the large bar next to the main pool.

People were starting to appear again now, as word was getting around that the incident was over and they were out of danger.

They went inside the bar, as it had been a little warm in the jungle and they had decided that a cool, air-conditioned room would be nice. A number of small tables were chosen and then pushed together to make a large table. The waiters were more than happy to help.

After getting comfortable, a round of drinks was ordered along with a few packets of nibbles.

"So, what happened? We were hoping we could scan the rebel for information," asked Kato.

"Well, me and Krissy went shopping and that was when he grabbed me," said Carina.

Carina and Datch then recounted the story. They reached the implosion of the shack and stopped.

"When you said 'pop,' you meant 'pop.'"

"Yes, the shack, rebel, and bomb all went 'pop!'"

"You do know you're not meant to use interspace missiles in an atmosphere, don't you?"

"You're not meant to use nuclear bombs in them either."

"Good point. How did you know the bomb wouldn't detonate?"

"Bombs explode, whereas interspace missiles implode. Therefore, we figured that if we detonated a missile next to the bomb, it couldn't explode because it was imploding."

"I can sort of see where the logic is in that. And it just vanished?"

"Yes, with a 'Pop!'"

"I wonder where it went?"

"Went?"

"Yes, the matter had to go somewhere. In space, the implosion is followed by an explosion."

"Oh. Well, it just went 'Pop.' We think they went to the star."

It should be noted that the atoms from the shack, rebel, and the bomb—what was left of them—were currently being nicely distributed around the star's photosphere.

"Then what happened?"

"We got up, dusted ourselves down, and came back here."

"Oh. Carina, are you sure he didn't say anything else to you?"

Carina sat and thought hard.

"I'm not sure, I think he may have mentioned a contact that had told him where we were. I've recorded it all with my implant. I can send it to the file if you like."

"That would be very helpful. Could you send it to my vid com please. We are currently doing a detailed assessment of all the staff and security service personnel in order to make sure we won't have any issues in the future."

"Ouch, that sounds painful?"

"It is, but it must be done to ensure the king's safety. He has tasked me and Tate to do it."

"Wow, now that does sound like a promotion," added Datch.

"The King said he knew he could trust us and felt we had the right skill set to do it."

Datch put up his hand and a waiter came over.

"Yes, Sir?" he said.

"Can we have the same again please?"

"Certainly, Sir. Do you require anything else?"

"Hmm, what entertainment do you have tonight?"

"We have a local pop band performing in the amphitheatre, Sir."

"Hmm, Folks, how about doing a few numbers to blow the cobwebs off and make everyone feel better?"

He looked around and there were a number of nods.

"Could you have a word with them and ask if they would mind if The Pack did a set on stage while they have their break between sets?"

"I can try, Sir."

"Thank you. If you could do that ASAP, please, as Timbo here will need to get the gear out of the back of the Raven. Oh, and add a fifty-credit tip on our bill for yourself."

"Thank you, Sir. I shall get right on it for you after I have brought you the drinks."

"Thank you."

"Datch, are you sure you want us to do a set?"

"Yes, it will be a warm-up gig for the weekend. Also, it will make the locals happy after we nearly blew up the planet."

Kato and the commander both raised an eyebrow.

"OK, but what numbers are we doing?"

"Wild Wind, Black Spiders Die, Hot City Nights, Planet Rock, Star Lovers, Green Gems, Music Warriors, and Supernova."

"OK, so eight then. What if they want more?"

"We'll have to talk to the other band."

The waiter came back with the drinks and then went off to talk to the manager.

"Kato, can you stop for the evening, or do you have to get back?" asked Rosey.

"We should really be getting back with all the information."

"What about our memory downloads? A member of the security services said we need to have them done." asked Datch.

"Oh. In which case I'll speak to them and ask if we can have a copy before we return home. That is if that's ok with you."

"Sure, maybe you can get them to do it in the morning. That way you could stop for the gig?"

"We'll head back to the ship and give them a call. I'll inform the palace of what has transpired as well as telling them we are waiting for a data download."

"Cool." said Datch.

With that, Kato and the commander got up and headed back to the Thoth ship. After an hour, the waiter came back and said that the manager had spoken to the band and they were happy to let "The Pack" do a set, saying it would be an honour to perform with them. The other band were called the Jungle Drums and would be setting up in around two hours.

It was decided that they would have another drink and then go and freshen up ready for the evening.

"The Pack" headed over to the amphitheatre to meet the Jungle Drums. They were a four-piece band with three men: one on drums, a bass guitarist, and a lead guitarist. They also had a female singer. They were a friendly bunch and were very pleased to meet "The Pack." They asked if they could have a picture with them on stage before they started, and they agreed.

They all headed over to the stage to take the picture and mark out their stage positions. Afterwards, Timbo went to fetch the gear. Once it was all sorted out, "The Pack" headed off to the restaurant to have a bite to eat.

Halfway through dinner, a man came in and spoke to one of the waiters before being shown over to them. He was introduced as the mayor of the village.

"Sorry to bother you all, but the security services told me about what has happened in the jungle. I understand you...erm, sorted the problem for us?" said the mayor.

"Yes, he was a rogue rebel who wanted to kill us along with quite a piece of your world," said Datch.

"Why?" asked the mayor.

"We helped stop an attempt to overthrow the King of Thoth. He was the last of the rebels."

"Oh, that explains the Thoth starship," said the mayor.

"Yes, they came when they heard he was here."

"Oh, good. What happened to him? The security services didn't say?"

"His atoms are now part of your star along with the shack and the nuclear bomb he had. So, all is good now. And if you want to stay around, we're having a party tonight to make everyone feel better."

"Oh. Nuclear bomb, you say?"

"Yes."

"And a party?"

"Yes."

"I'll just...erm, call my wife."

"You can ask the whole village to come if you like. Once-in-a-lifetime opportunity to see 'The Pack' perform live for free."

"What time does it start?"

"In about two hours."

"I'll see what I can do. Thank you for seeing me."

"You're welcome."

With that, the mayor turned around and headed off back to the village.

The Pack sat chilling, and then Hagger spoke.

"Err, we don't have a dressing room."

"It's thirty-four degrees outside, and we're doing an impromptu open-air gig. You really want a dressing room?" said Tank.

"I was thinking about the drinks!"

"We have a bar next to the stage, and I'm sure the waiters will be more than happy to fetch them for you," added Dapo.

Hagger looked at them.

"OK. But I want my drinks cold."

"I'll make sure they are cold for you," said Datch, and half smiled and half grinned.

'I spotted that grin,' came Carina's voice in his head.

Datch just turned to her and smiled.

They finished their food, and Timbo went off to make sure everything was ready, while the rest of them had another couple of drinks. Then it was time to go to the back of the stage to wait with the other band.

At the back of the stage was the waiting area. It was not a dressing room, or even a room, come to that, but more of an outside area with seats and a couple of tables. Timbo was standing next to a hastily constructed large table, and he had got a round of drinks ready for them.

Around the front of the stage, the amphitheatre was starting to fill up with people. It looked like it could hold about seven or eight hundred, and judging by the influx of people, it was going to be full.

The other band were very friendly, and they started chatting to them, asking what it was like to be megastars.

"Megastars? When did that happen?" asked Hagger.

"I'm not sure, it must have been at one of the after parties," said Dapo.

"You guys really don't think about it, do you?" said the lead guitarist, who was called Cane.

"No. We just have fun," said Carina.

"Doesn't the long trips away from your families make you homesick?" asked the lead singer, Lari.

"No, we are a family. We have been since we got together ten years ago. Yes, our parents live on Bellatrix, and we see them for about fourteen months out of the year, so being away for the other six months is not bad."

"Yes, and we get to see a lot of the galaxy in the process," added Krissy.

"I bet you play all the best places in the galaxy. What's your favourite?" asked Lari.

"The Barbers Inn on Bellatrix."

"The Barbers Inn?"

"It was where we started, and we play there every week when we're at home. It's only a small bar by city standards, and it only holds about the same number of people as this place, but we like it. We hang out there a lot as well, and we have our own table upstairs."

"Wow, sounds very cool."

Cane looked at the clock that was hanging on a post next to the steps leading up to the side of the stage.

"Looks like it's nearly time."

"Err, just to let you know, you might start sparkling after we start. It's nothing to worry about, okay?"

"Okay."

The Jungle Drums got ready and waited at the top of the steps. Datch looked at them and remembered the days when they waited with anticipation for Jim to call them onto the stage at the Barbers. Now it was normal to them, but back then it was magical.

"What's up, Datch?" asked Fred, noticing the look on Datch's face.

"I was just thinking about when we waited like that in the Barbers. How things have changed."

"Yes, they have a bit, but we still manage to get into trouble." He laughed.

"Err, can we do Star Lovers with Krissy up front?" asked Carina.

"If you like, but let's do that say halfway through. Krissy, you okay with that?" asked Datch.

"Err, yes, but which bit do I do?"

"Just do the chorus to start with and then follow my lead."

"Okay."

The Pack watched as the Jungle Drums ran on stage.

They heard Lari say on the mic, "Hello folks! Do we have a night for you tonight? We're kicking things off and then we have the Galactic Mega Band, The Pack performing for you. So, let's get this show on the road."

They went straight into the first song. The Pack sat and listened as the Jungle Drums played song after song. They got to the seventh song and Datch stood up.

"OK, folks, party time." He held out his hand. The others stood up and placed their hands on top of his.

"One, two, three, let's party!" They pushed down before springing up with their hands and then heading up to the side of the stage.

The Jungle Drums finished their last song and Lira looked at The Pack waiting at the side. Datch nodded to her.

"OK, it's now time for our very special guests. Let's hear it for The Pack!"

There was a big roar from the crowd and The Pack came running on the stage.

"Hello Hybaysus!" shouted Datch. The crowd roared again. He turned to Tish and nodded.

"Wild Wind" blasted out and The Pack's gems energized. The columns of green energy formed around them and then started to build in intensity. Then a ring of energy expanded, filling the amphitheatre with a green glow. Sparkles appeared around the members of the crowd and everyone started smiling and dancing.

Then it was time for "Star Lovers" and Krissy came forward and stood between them. Datch and Carina started to sing to each other and kept coming back to the centre of the stage for the chorus. Then all three of them came together for the kiss. Their auras combined and then exploded across the amphitheatre, sweeping out into the jungle.

The Jungle Drums, who were watching from the wings, looked at themselves and realized they were dancing and sparkling. The music was taking control of them.

The songs continued, one after another. Then came "Music Warriors." Datch looked at the Jungle Drums. They were dancing away at the side of the stage. "Supernova" was next up and Datch waved at the Jungle Drums to come on stage. The guitarists joined Datch and Dapo, and the lead singer joined Carina. The drummer fell in with the bikers.

The stage became one big party. Supernova turned in "Space Dust" and then "Rocking the City," "Someone to Love," "No Place to Hide," "Shoot for the Stars," and finally finished with "We Can't Get High Enough." Timbo put some party music on the PA system and The Pack and the Jungle Drums went to join the crowd. It was gone one in the morning when they left to go to bed.

The next morning, the commando squad and Carina had their implant data downloads and the security services confirmed the events. Kato was given a copy and the Thoth ship left for home.

The rest of the week passed by with The Pack chilling out and signing the odd autograph. The weekend arrived and it was time to leave.

The Pack boarded the Raven. Datch and Clax did the pre-flight checks.

"OK, folks," said Datch, turning to the others. "Time to hit the road."

He turned to the front.

"Hybaysus control, this is Raven ready to depart for Klayton."

"Raven, you are cleared for launch. Traffic is light at the moment. Lock on to beacon 2234HYB for orbital intersect and then you are cleared for free space exit."

"Locking on to beacon."

Datch brought the main engines online and the Raven took to the sky.

The End

Other Books in the Chronicles of Datch Series.

Datch – The Great Adventure.

The Datch Pack.

The Mystical Gem.

Arcaneus.

The Quest for Earthly Delights.

The Orphaned World.

www.ingramcontent.com/pod-product-compliance
Lightning Source LLC
Chambersburg PA
CBHW070618170726
48291CB00003B/793